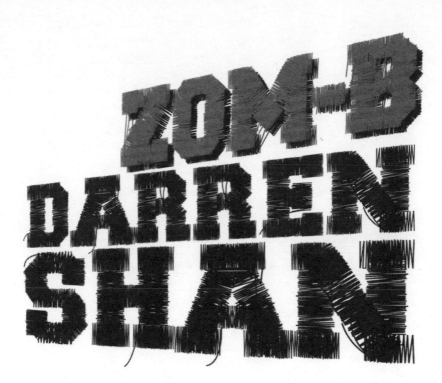

ZOM-B

DARREN SHAN

SIMON AND SCHUSTER

First published in Great Britain in 2012 by Simon & Schuster UK Ltd
A CBS COMPANY

1 3 5 7 9 10 8 6 4 2

Simon & Schuster UK Ltd
1st Floor
222 Gray's Inn Road
London
WC1X 8HB

www.simonandschuster.co.uk

Simon & Schuster Australia, Sydney
Simon & Schuster India, New Delhi

A CIP catalogue copy for this book
is available from the British Library.

HB ISBN: 978-0-85707-752-3
EBOOK ISBN: 978-0-85707-755-4
TPB ISBN: 978-0-85707-753-0

Printed and bound by CPI Group (UK) Ltd, Croydon, CR0 4YY

For:
Zom-Bas, my undead lass!

OBE (Order of the Bloody Entrails) to:
Laura Zi Giuseppe, for a brace of
carefully coordinated Irish jobs!

Dead good editors: Venetia GoZling
and Kate Zullivan

My heart goes out, as always,
to the ChriZtopher Little brainiacs

THEN . . .

It was the darkest, most wretched hour of the night when the dead came back to life and spread like a plague of monstrous locusts through the village of Pallaskenry. The luckier victims were slaughtered in their sleep, their skulls ripped open, their brains devoured. The others suffered a far more terrible fate.

The living and the undead shared the village for a short, frantic time, but it was a balance made in hell and it could not last. One side would surely wipe out the other. As the demented, demonic beasts tore into their unsuspecting prey, killing or infecting, it soon became apparent that this was a war the living had never been destined to win.

*

Brian Barry watched sickly as his mother dug through the shredded remains of her husband's face to scoop out his brains. Mum had often joked about killing Brian's dad, on nights when he had stumbled home from the local pub, or when he wouldn't shut up about football. Brian and his dad had always laughed when she made her outlandish threats. But neither was laughing now.

Brian couldn't understand how the world had changed so abruptly. It had been an ordinary Sunday night. He'd watched some TV, finished his homework just before going to bed, and settled down for a night of sweet dreams before another school week kicked off.

Screams had disturbed his slumber. Brian wasn't a light sleeper, but even the dead were unable to sleep through the uproar in Pallaskenry that night.

Brian had thought at first that somebody was throwing a party. But he lived on a quiet stretch of road. His neighbours weren't party animals. Had teenagers driven out from Limerick city to bring noise and chaos to the countryside?

As his head cleared and he turned on the light in his bedroom, he quickly realised that this was no party. The screams were genuine roars of terror. Looking out of his window, he spotted some of his neighbours running, shrieking, fighting. He watched, awestruck, as Mrs Shanahan stabbed one of her sons in the chest with a long, sharp knife, then staggered away, keening sharply.

The stabbed son should have died instantly, as the knife had pierced his heart. But to Brian's astonishment he yanked out the knife, tossed it aside, then fell upon his mother with a bloodthirsty howl. Mrs Shanahan had time to scream once more. Then her son somehow cracked her head open with his fingers and began pulling out lumps of her brain.

Brian turned away and vomited as Mrs Shanahan's son stuffed bits of his dead mother's brain into his mouth and swallowed gleefully. Then Brian rushed to his mum and dad's room to seek protection.

They weren't there.

As if in a nightmare, Brian shuffled towards the kitchen, where he could see a light. Pushing open the door, he spotted his parents, but he didn't call out to them. There was no point, he saw that immediately. His father would never hear anything again. His face had been ripped apart and his body was deathly still.

As for Brian's mother, she was too busy eating her dead husband's brain to care about anything her son might have to say. There was a nasty cut on her left arm and a green fungus was creeping across the wound.

There was something strange about her teeth and fingers too, but Brian didn't focus on those details. He could stomach no more. Weeping softly, he backed away from the kitchen of death and fled into the night of blood and screams.

Brian headed for the main street of Pallaskenry, crying, moaning, shivering. He could see atrocities unravelling wherever he looked, corpses littering the road, people – neighbours, family members, friends – feasting on the dead, tucking into their brains.

Fighting was rife, brother struggling with sister, wife with husband, child with parent. It made no sense. It was as if a great madness had swept through the village and struck at random. Anyone who tried to reason with the cannibalistic crazies was knocked down and ripped apart. The only ones who stood any chance of survival were those who didn't stop to ask questions, who didn't try to help, who simply turned tail and ran.

But Brian was a child and he believed that adults had all the answers, that you should always seek assistance if you found yourself in trouble. So he pushed on, searching for a police officer, a teacher, a priest . . . *anyone.*

All he found was more horror, blood everywhere, corpses everywhere, undead monsters everywhere.

Nobody could help Brian Barry. It was every man, woman and child for themselves.

Brian somehow made it to the top of the main street, ducking challenges, skipping past the lunges of blood-thirsty abominations. In the middle of the killing frenzy there was no shortage of targets, so the undead creatures didn't take much notice of an eleven-year-old boy.

At the top of the street, where the road branched, a man was standing, feet spread wide apart, hands on hips, studying the violence. Lots of undead creatures were gathered at this point, scrapping with the living or feeding on the brains of the freshly killed. None attacked the man in the middle of the road. Some growled suspiciously at him, but all of the monsters let him be.

Brian was young, but he was no fool. He saw his best chance of survival and launched himself at it, desperation lending him one last blast of speed when he'd been sure that his lungs were about to burst.

Slipping past the frenzied, shark-like killers, Brian threw himself at the feet of the man who was immune to the attacks. He looked up and got ready to beg for his life. But when he saw the man's face, he paused. The tall man was very thin, with a large potbelly and extraordinarily unsettling eyes. They were double the size of

Brian's, the largest eyes the boy had ever seen, unnaturally white, with a tiny dark pupil set in the centre of each. Brian was immediately put in mind of an owl.

'Yes, little boy?' the man murmured. He had a soft, pleasant voice, like one of the announcers on the TV shows which Brian had been watching earlier that night. It didn't really suit those eerie eyes.

'Please,' Brian gasped, grabbing hold of the man's legs. 'Help me. Please. My dad's dead. My mum . . .'

'She killed him?' the man asked, then tutted when Brian nodded. 'How sad that you had to bear witness to such a shocking scene. No child should ever be put in so unfortunate a situation. You have my condolences.'

One of the undead creatures darted at them, reaching for Brian, drooling as it moved in for the kill.

'Back!' the man with the large eyes barked. The monster snarled at him, but retreated as ordered.

'You . . . you can . . . help me?' Brian wheezed.

The man frowned. 'I could, but with so many in your perilous position, it hardly seems fair that I should single you out for special treatment.'

'Please!' Brian wailed, clutching the tall man's legs even tighter. 'I didn't do anything wrong. I don't want to die. *Please!*

The man sighed and looked around at the dead, the

dying and the undead. He hesitated, then decided to be merciful. 'Very well,' he muttered. 'But I'll only do it for you. The others will have to fend for themselves. What is your name?'

'Brian Barry.'

'You need to let go of my legs, Brian, move back and kneel in front of me.'

'Kneel?' Brian echoed uncertainly.

'Yes,' the man said. 'Then close your eyes and say a silent prayer, any prayer will do, or none at all if you're not religious, although I find that even the most agnostic individual gains a measure of comfort from prayer at a time like this.'

'You'll help me if I kneel and pray?' Brian asked.

'Yes,' the man smiled, and although it was a cold smile, it filled the boy with hope.

'OK,' Brian said, releasing the man's legs. The undead noticed this and started to move in for the kill. Brian gulped, then closed his eyes and prayed manically. He couldn't remember the words very well, but he did the best he could, trying not to think about his mum and dad and how he used to complain when they took him to church.

The tall man looked down tenderly on the boy. Then he spotted the monsters closing in and wiped the smile

away. He would have to act swiftly if he was to honour his promise and spare the boy the agony of death at the hands of these foul beasts.

'You have been a brave boy, Brian,' the man whispered. 'I am sure you will be reunited with your parents in the next world.'

Then his hands snaked out. Brian didn't see the long, bony fingers, and only barely felt them as they gripped his head and twisted left then right. He heard a sharp cracking noise, but felt no pain and was dead before he knew it.

The man let the corpse drop and bade Brian a silent farewell as the living dead moved in and tore into the boy's skull. He watched for a while, then checked his watch and grunted. There was still a long way to go until morning.

With a small cough, he adjusted the ends of his sleeves, then started down the road into the village, leaving the undead leeches to carve up Brian Barry's skull and feast upon the hot, sweet brain within.

NOW . . .

ONE

Zombies my arse! I've got a *real* problem on my hands. Dad's been drinking and I can tell by his beady eyes that he's close to tipping over the edge.

We've been watching the news, a report about the alleged zombie attack in Ireland. Dad takes a swig of cider, then snorts and switches channels.

'I was watching that,' Mum complains.

'You're not any more,' Dad grunts.

'But it's important,' Mum presses. 'They might attack here. We need to know what to do, Todd.'

'B knows what to do, don't you?' Dad says, winking at me, and it's a relief to see he's still at the stage where he can crack a joke.

'Of course,' I grin. 'Put my head between my legs and kiss my arse goodbye!'

We crack up laughing. Mum tuts and pulls a face. She doesn't like it when we swear. She thinks foul language is a sign of ill-breeding. I don't know how she ended up with Dad—he could swear for a living.

'Don't be silly, Daisy,' Dad says. 'It's all a con. Zombies? The dead returning to life to feast on the living? Pull the other one.'

'But it's on the *news*,' Mum says. 'They showed pictures.'

'They can do anything with computers these days,' Dad says. 'I bet B could knock up something just as realistic on our laptop. Am I right, B?'

'Dead on,' I nod. 'With a few apps, I could out-zombie George Romero.'

'Who's that?' Mum frowns.

'The president of South Africa,' Dad says seriously and we both howl at her bewildered expression.

'It's all very well for the pair of you to laugh like hyenas,' Mum snaps, face reddening. 'But what happens if zombies attack us here? You won't be laughing if they kill me and B.'

'I'll happily chuck *you* to them if you keep on

16

moaning,' Dad says, and there's an edge to his voice now, one I'm all too familiar with.

Dad stares at Mum, his eyes hard. I tense, waiting for him to roar, or maybe just throw a punch at her without warning. If he does, I'll hurl myself at him, the way I have countless times in the past. I love him, but I love Mum too, and I can never stand by and let him wade into her. The trouble is there's not much I can do to stop him. We could both be in for some serious battering tonight.

But instead, after a dangerous pause, Dad smirks and switches back to the news. That's Dad all over—unpredictable as the weather.

I scratch the back of my head – I had it shaved tight at the weekend and it's always itchy for a few days when I do that – and watch the footage from Ireland. It's a helicopter shot. They're flying over Pallaskenry, the small village where zombies apparently ran wild on Sunday.

The village is in ruins. Buildings are being burnt to the ground by soldiers with cool-looking flame-throwers. Corpses all over the place. At least they *look* like corpses. Dad reckons they're dummies. 'That's a waste of good ketchup,' he said when Mum challenged him about the blood.

'I mean,' Dad says as we watch, 'if it had happened in London, fair enough, I might believe it. But bloody Ireland? It's one of their Paddy jokes. *There was an Englishman, an Irishman and a zombie . . .*'

'But they've shown dead people,' Mum persists. 'They've interviewed some of the survivors who got out.'

'Never heard of actors?' Dad says witheringly, then turns to me. 'You don't buy any of this, do you?'

'Not a word.' I point at the TV. They're showing a clip that's already passed into legend on YouTube. One of the zombies is biting into a woman's head. He's a guy in pyjamas. His eyes are crazy and he's covered in blood, but apart from that you wouldn't look at him twice in a crowd. The woman screams as he chews off a chunk of her skull and digs his fingers into her brain. As he pulls out a handful and stuffs it into his mouth, the camera pans away and, if you listen closely, you can hear the cameraman vomiting.

The clip had gone viral by Monday morning, but they first showed it on TV that evening. There was uproar the next day, papers saying it shouldn't have been aired, people getting their knickers in a right old twist. It gave me a fright when I first saw it. Dad too, even if he won't admit it. Now it's just a bit of fun. Like when you see a horror film more than once—scary the first time, but the more you watch it, the lamer it gets.

'He should have dipped that bit of brain in curry sauce,' I joke.

'B!' Mum gasps. 'Don't joke about it!'

'Why not?' I retort. 'None of it's real. I reckon it's a trailer for a new movie. You wait, another few days and they'll admit it was a publicity stunt. Anyone who fell for it will look a right idiot, won't they?'

'But the police and soldiers . . .' On the TV, a tank fires at a church, blasting holes out of the walls, exposing zombies who were sheltering inside—these guys are like vampires, they don't come out much in the day.

'They're part of the campaign,' I insist. 'They've been paid to go along with the act.'

Mum frowns. 'Surely they'd get in trouble if they lied to the public like that.'

'Trouble's like a bad stink,' Dad says. 'Throw enough money at it and nobody cares. Any lawyers who go after these guys will be given a big fat cheque and that'll be the end of that.'

'I dunno,' Mum says, shaking her head. 'They're talking about a curfew here.'

'Course they are,' Dad sneers, knocking back another

slug of cider. 'The government would love that. Get everyone off the streets, terrify us into holing up like rats. It'd leave them free to do whatever they wanted at night. They'd ship in more immigrants while we weren't watching. That might be what the whole thing's about, a plot to make us look away while they sneak in a load of scabs who'll work for peanuts and steal our jobs.'

Mum looks dubious. 'You can't be serious, Todd.'

'I'd bet my crown jewels on it,' he says firmly.

She stares at him, maybe wondering how she ended up marrying such a paranoid nutter. Or maybe she's trying to convince herself that he's right, to avoid any arguments and associated beatings.

The worst thing about this zombie scare is talk of a curfew. I'd go mad if I had to stay home every night, locked in with Mum and Dad. I mean, most nights I stay in anyway, watching TV, surfing the web, playing computer games, listening to music. But I know that I *can* go out, any time I please. Take that choice away and I'd be no better off than a prisoner.

I shiver at the thought of being caged up and get to my feet. 'I've had enough of zombies. They're boring me. I'm heading out.'

'I'm not sure that's a good idea,' Mum says. 'What if there's an attack?'

'Don't be daft,' I laugh.

'But if they struck there, they could strike here. We're not that far from Ireland.' She looks like she's about to cry. 'They come out at night, the reporters all say so. If they attack London and catch you on the street . . .'

'Dad?' I look to him for support.

'I dunno . . .' he mutters, and for the first time I see that he's not so sure that this is the work of sneaky liberals.

'Don't tell me you're gonna start too,' I groan.

Dad chews the inside of his cheek, the way he does when he's thinking hard.

'Put your foot down, Todd,' Mum says. 'It's dangerous out there. You can't –'

'I can do whatever the bloody hell I want!' Dad shouts. 'Don't tell me what I can and can't do.'

'I'm not,' Mum squeaks. 'I was only –'

'Shut it,' Dad says quietly and Mum zips up immediately. She knows that tone. We both do. I gulp as Dad sits forward, putting down the can of cider. He cracks his fingers, eyeballing Mum. She's trembling. She's not the sharpest tool in the box. She missed the earlier warning signs, his expression, the clip to his words. But now she's up to speed. Dad's in a foul mood. There could be some thuggery on the cards tonight.

I start to edge towards Mum, to do my best to protect her. I hate it when Dad hits me. But I hate it even
more when he hits her. Mum's soft. I'm more like Dad,
a tough little nut. I'll distract him if I can, draw his
attention away from Mum. If I'm lucky, he'll only slap
me. If not, and he starts punching and kicking, I'll curl
up into a ball and take it. Won't be the first time. Won't
be the last. Better he does it to me than Mum.

'B!' Dad barks, making me jump.

'Yeah?' I croak, trying not to shake.

He glares at me—then snorts, picks up the can of
cider and settles back again. 'Go do whatever the hell
you feel like.'

'Sure thing, boss,' I smile and tip him a stupid
salute.

Dad smirks. 'You're an idiot,' he says.

'I know where I get it from,' I chuck back at him,
feeling safe enough to wind him up a bit. I can do that
to Dad when he's in the right mood. He's a great laugh
when he wants to be.

'Oi!' he roars and throws a cushion at me.

I laugh and duck out, knowing Mum will be fine
now, delighted at this unexpected swing, feeling on top
of the world. There's nothing sweeter than a narrow
escape. I don't know why Dad laid off at the last

moment, and I don't try to figure it out. I gave up trying to read his mind years ago.

The last thing I see is Mum getting up to retrieve the cushion. Dad doesn't like it if she leaves stuff lying around. Doesn't matter if he left it there. Cleaning up is *her* job.

TWO

Out of the flat, down three flights of stairs, taking the steps two at a time, four on the last set. I slap the wall on my right as I fly past. Someone spray-painted a giant arse on it months ago and I always slap it for good luck when I pass. Some of the neighbours have tried scrubbing it off, but it's hanging in there, faded but defiant. I love graffiti. If I could paint, I'd be out covering the walls of London every night.

I land like a cat, cool in my new, totally black trainers. There was a bit of red running through them when they first came out of their box, and the brand name shone brightly, but I carefully went over everything with a heavy-duty Sharpie. B Smith is nobody's advertising pawn!

It's not yet six, plenty of daylight left. I don't know what Mum was panicking about. Even if zombies were real, and even if they did attack here, they wouldn't show their faces for another hour, not if the news teams have got it right.

I check myself out in shop windows. Plain black T-shirt and jeans, no tags to show what make they are, threadbare in places, but worn in naturally by me, none of your bloody designer wear and tear.

I'm almost past Black Spot when I stop and back-track. Vinyl's in there with his old man. Black Spot is a retro freak's paradise. They only stock vinyl records, along with clothes, toys, hats and other bits and pieces from the dark ages. I even saw a video recorder in the window once.

Vinyl's dad loves all that twentieth-century crap. He won't let CDs or DVDs in his house, and as for downloads, forget it! They have a computer, but all the music sites on it are blocked. He says the crackle of old records is what real music is all about, that digital tracks don't make the air throb.

I lean close to the window and tap on it softly. Vinyl looks up and scowls. He hates it when we spot him with his dad. Vinyl's old man is all right – he does his own thing and doesn't make a song and dance about it – but he's a weirdo. I think Vinyl secretly likes the records which his dad makes him listen to, but he never admits that to us or defends his dad when we slag him off. As long as we don't take it too far. I started to make a joke once about his dad liking the small holes that you find in the middle of records. Vinyl very quietly told me to shut up. He didn't have to say any more. I'm not afraid of Vinyl, but I know he'd wipe the floor with me if we fought. Why sign up for a beating if you don't have to?

I pull a face and stick out my tongue. Vinyl gives me the finger, then says something to his dad. Old man Vinyl looks up, nods at me and smiles. I salute him, the same way I saluted Dad a while ago. Vinyl comes out, nudging the door open with his head.

'You're so cool,' I gush, squeezing my hands together and making doe eyes at him.

'Get stuffed,' Vinyl sneers.

We grin and knock knuckles.

'I like the hair,' Vinyl says. 'Number 3?'

'Sod that. Number 2.'

'Hardcore.'

Vinyl's got long, curly hair. He'd love to shave it, but his mum would cry and he doesn't want to upset her. He's a soft git, Vinyl. But hard when he needs to be.

There aren't many who get the better of him in a punch-up.

'How's the new school?' I ask.

Vinyl rolls his eyes. 'I should have failed that bloody test.'

'Bad?' I laugh.

'You wouldn't believe it.'

Vinyl took a Mensa test in the summer. Turned out he's smarter than the rest of us put together. His mum went gaga – she thinks he's the new Einstein – and begged him to switch to a posh school. He hated bailing on us, but she turned on the tears and he caved.

'What's it really like?' I ask as we stroll, punching each other's arm every now and then.

'All right,' he shrugs. 'I thought they'd be full of themselves, but most aren't much different to us. I'm doing OK, not the best, not the worst.'

'What about the teachers?'

He shrugs again. 'They wouldn't last long in our place. I'd give them a week—they'd be headcases after that.'

Vinyl still thinks he's one of us. And at the moment he is. But that will change. You can't switch schools and carry on as if nothing's happened. He'll make new friends soon and start hanging out with them. Another few weeks and we won't see a lick of him. Way of the world.

'You must be crapping yourself,' I tell him.

'What are you talking about?' he frowns.

'The zombies.'

'What about them?'

'They go for freaks with big brains.'

He laughs sarcastically. 'Know what I like about you, B?'

'What?'

'You'll be dead one day.'

We snicker, knock knuckles and head for the park.

THREE

Some of the gang are already in the park, as I guessed they would be. We're too young to get into pubs and there's not much else to do around here. They're hanging out by the swings, trying to look cool. Dipsticks! I mean, how the hell are you supposed to look cool in a *park*?

'Strewth, it's the B-ster,' Trev hoots. 'And who's that with our cheery chum? Strike me pink if it ain't our old mate Vinyl! Evening, guv'nor.'

Trev loves a bit of mockney. Sometimes it's funny, but it gets stale quick.

'Anything happening?' I ask, taking one of the swings and lifting my feet up so that everyone can admire my trainers.

'Sod all,' Copper says.

'Looking for zombies,' Kray yawns.

'We thought Vinyl was one of them,' Ballydefeck says.

'Eat me,' Vinyl retorts.

'I wouldn't even if I was a zombie,' Ballydefeck sniffs.

'Anyone else coming?' I ask.

Trev shrugs. 'Talk of a curfew has scared a lot of people. I'm not expecting many more. Surprised to see you, B. I thought you'd have been kept in.'

'It'd take more than the threat of a few zombies to keep *me* in,' I sneer.

'Aren't you afraid of the living dead?' Kray asks.

'I'm more afraid of your killer breath.'

Laughter all round. I grin and treat myself to a swing. It's great to have friends to slag off.

Copper produces a packet of fags and passes them round. He's good that way. He'd share his last butt with you. He used to take a lot of flak for being a ginger before he butched up, but I always liked him. I slagged him off, sure – and I gave him his nickname – but in a nice way.

I've given a few of my friends nicknames over the years. I'm good at it. You'd be amazed how some people struggle. It doesn't take a stroke of genius to look at a redhead and call him Copper, but even that simple task is beyond a lot of the kids I know.

I'm prouder of Ballydefeck. His family's Irish. Most of us have a bit of Paddy in our blood, but his lot act like they still live in the bog, spuds for dinner every night of the week, Irish dancing competitions at the weekend, Daniel O'Donnell blasting out loud in every room of their house if you pop round. He was known as Paddy or Mick for years. Then one night I was watching a rerun of *Father Ted* and I came up with Ballydefeck. He's answered to that ever since.

Kray digs out an iPod with a plug-in speaker. It's brand new, the latest model. I whistle appreciatively. 'Fall off the back of a lorry?' I ask.

'I don't know what you mean,' Kray says indignantly, but his smirk ruins his show of innocence. We've all nicked a bit in our time, but Kray would have been Fagin's star pupil.

We listen to some good tunes – Kray has great taste – and talk about TV, zombies, music, sex. Vinyl tells us about the girls in his new school. He says they're hot and easy. Trev, Copper and Ballydefeck listen with their mouths open as he describes what he's been getting up to with them. Me and Kray look at each other and roll our eyes—we know bullshit when we smell it. But we don't tell Vinyl to shut up. It's fun listening to him stringing the fools along.

After a while I spot a skinny black teenager entering the park. It's Tyler, a kid from our year. He stops when he sees us, hesitates, then backs up.

'Tyler!' I shout. 'Get your arse over here!'

He grins nervously and taps his watch. Vanishes before I can call to him again.

'A pity,' I sneer. 'I fancied a lynching.'

'That's a bit harsh, isn't it?' Vinyl says.

'Only joking,' I reply.

'Tyler's all right,' Vinyl mutters.

'No, he's not,' I growl.

'What's wrong with him?' Vinyl challenges me, then smiles with icy sweetness before I can answer. 'It's not the colour of his skin, is it?'

I scowl at Vinyl, but don't say anything. Because to an extent he's right. Dad's a racist and proud of it. He hates anyone who isn't from England, especially if they're dark-skinned. In his ideal world the ruling party would be the Ku Klux Klan and he'd go riding through the streets of London on a horse every day with a load of hood-wearing buddies, keeping law and order with a thick length of rope.

Dad's always warning me of the dangers of racial

tolerance. He pushes Aryan books and pamphlets my way. The first picture book I remember reading by myself featured a family of naughty golliwogs.

I don't believe the same things that Dad does. I don't want to be like him, not that way. But at the same time I've got to live with him. I learnt early on not to challenge his word. So I put up with the ranting and raving. I read the hate lit. I laugh at his crude jokes. I've even gone to a few meetings with him, rooms full of angry white men muttering bloody murder.

The trouble with putting on an act is that sometimes it's hard to tell where the actor stops and the real you begins. It's rubbed off on me to an extent, the years of pretending to hate. Vinyl's black as the ace of spades, but he's my only coloured friend. And it's not just because I know Dad would hit the roof if he saw me hanging out with black kids or Asians. Part of me genuinely fears the menace of those who are different. I've read so much and heard so much and been forced to say so much that sometimes I forget that I don't believe it.

To be honest, I'm amazed I'm still friends with Vinyl. We hung out together when we were tiny, before I started selecting my associates more cautiously. When Dad beat me a few times, and told me to stop having anything to do with *that horrible little black kid*, that should have been the end of it. I tried to avoid Vinyl after that, but I couldn't. We got on too well. He made me laugh, he never teased me, I could talk to him about anything.

I learnt to sneak behind Dad's back, never mention Vinyl at home, not be seen with him close to where we live. He's my secret friend. If Dad knew, he'd knock the stuffing out of me. Even one black friend is one too many as far as he's concerned.

'Come on,' Vinyl says again, bristling now. 'What's wrong with Tyler?'

'I don't like his face,' I snap. 'What difference does it make?'

'I ran into your dad a few days ago,' Vinyl says. 'He recognised me, which was a surprise. I thought we all looked the same to him.'

'Hey,' Trev says uneasily. 'Let's drop it.'

'He told me he'd heard about my new school,' Vinyl goes on, ignoring Trev and staring hard at me. 'Said it was amazing what they could teach chimps these days. Asked me if I could peel my own bananas now.'

I feel my face flush. I'm ashamed of my mean-spirited, foul-mouthed father. But I'm even more ashamed of myself, because I instinctively want to

36

defend him. I know it's wrong. He shouldn't have said that to Vinyl – to anyone – but part of me wants to take his side, because no matter what, he's my dad and I love him.

'I can't control what he says,' I mutter, dropping my gaze.

'But do you agree with it?' Vinyl growls.

'Of course not!' I spit. 'Tyler's a whiny brat. He gets up my nose. It's got nothing to do with him being black.'

Vinyl eyes me coldly for a long, probing moment. Then he relaxes. 'That's all right then.' He winks. 'You should tell your dad that you want to move in with me.'

'Wishful thinking!' I snort.

We laugh, knock knuckles and everything's OK again. In a weird, messed-up, uncomfortable kind of way. It's not easy sometimes, having a racist for a dad.

FOUR

We meet Suze and La Lips outside a kebab shop. They're sharing a bag of chips and Suze has a doner that she's saving for later.

'Lovely ladies!' Trev croons. 'What does a guy have to do to get a chip and a kiss around here?'

'Sod off,' Suze growls as he drapes an arm round each of them. La Lips smiles and cuddles into him.

'What's up?' I ask, eyeing the chips hungrily. I had dinner before I came out, but I always get the munchies when I spy a bag of steaming hot chips.

'We were meant to be meeting Elephant and Stagger Lee, but they never turned up,' La Lips pouts.

'What are you doing with them?' Copper asks

suspiciously. La Lips has kissed just about every boy she's ever come into contact with – I snogged her too, a while back, to see what it was like, though she tells me to shut my trap whenever I bring that up – but Copper has been sort of going steady with her for the last few weeks.

'Stagger Lee was going to give us new ringtones for our phones,' Suze says.

'More Nick Cave I bet,' Copper scowls (Stagger Lee's a Nick Cave freak—he was nicknamed after one of the singer's most famous songs) and drags La Lips away from Trev.

'Careful!' she shouts, spilling a couple of chips. She rubs her arm where he pinched her and glares.

'You won't be copping a feel tonight,' Kray laughs.

'He doesn't cop a feel *any* night,' La Lips says, tossing her hair indignantly, but nobody buys that for even a second.

'Here,' Suze says, handing me the bag of chips. 'I can't bear to look at you drooling any longer.'

'Cheers, ears.' I tuck in and the others crowd round me. Thirty seconds later the chips are gone and we're licking our lips.

Suze shakes her head. 'Like a pack of dogs,' she sighs. Then she smiles at Vinyl, the only one who didn't grab any chips. 'How's the new school?'

Vinyl shrugs. 'You know. All right.'

'Is it very different to ours?' La Lips asks.

'Yeah. They have gold-rimmed toilet seats.'

'No way!' she gasps.

Everyone laughs.

'You're an idiot,' I tell her.

'Less of that,' Copper says, draping a protective arm round her.

'My hero,' La Lips simpers and stands on her toes to stick her tongue down his throat.

'Not in public!' I roar and we push on down the street, jostling and laughing.

The girls don't have much news. They're as bored as we are. Suze and I walk a little ahead of the others, chatting about our mums—they used to be best friends when they were our age. But then Ballydefeck starts telling us to kiss each other, so I round on him and give him a slap to shut him up. He covers his head with both hands. 'Not the face, B! Not the face!' In the end I kick him playfully and leave it at that.

We come to an off-licence and pause by the window, enviously studying the bottles. Most of us have had a drink or two in our time – Dad let me sip beer when I was a baby, for laughs – but it's hard to get hold of. Another few years and we'll be able to pass for eighteen and go to parties and drink ourselves stupid. But for now we can't do much apart from ogle and dream.

'Wait here,' I tell the others, deciding to stir things up a bit. I push into the shop and walk straight to the beer fridge. I pick up a six-pack of the cheapest brand I can find – in case I get lucky – then lug it to the counter. The Pakistani guy behind the till stares at me, unimpressed. 'Ring it up, boss,' I tell him.

'You are underage.' He doesn't even ask to see my ID.

'No, I'm not. Go on, ring it up, I'm good for it.' I dig out a tattered wallet which once belonged to my dad and slide out a tenner which I've been holding onto since Friday.

'You are underage,' he says again. 'It is illegal to sell alcohol to anyone under the age of eighteen. Please leave my shop immediately.'

'*Please leave my shop immediately*,' I echo, mimicking his accent. I know it's petty, but I can't stop myself.

'If you do not leave, I will call the police,' he says.

'Call them what?' I smirk.

He points to a security camera. 'This is all being recorded. I would advise you to return the alcohol to its shelf and –'

I let the six-pack drop. The cans fizz but don't explode. 'Stick them back on the shelf yourself, numbnuts.'

His face darkens and he leans forward to strike me. Then he stops and points at the door. 'Out!' he screams.

I laugh and shoot him the finger. I give the finger to the camera too, then take my time heading for the door. I plan to tell Dad about this later, knowing he'll laugh, lovingly run his hand over my head and tell me I did good.

'You're crazy,' Kray yells when I get outside, then he bangs my knuckles hard. They're all laughing and Trev gives me knuckles too.

'Same old B,' Vinyl smiles tightly. For a moment I think he's going to have a go at me again, but he says nothing more.

'You didn't really expect him to sell you any beer, did you?' Suze asks.

'No.' I whip out a bar of chocolate from beneath my T-shirt. 'But he was so wound-up about the beer, he never saw me palming this.'

Lots of cheers. They all lean in for a square. I push them away, then dole it out, a piece for everyone, a quick prayer of thanks to Mr Cadbury, then on we go, the others still cooing over what I did.

Later I head home alone through the dark. And do I worry about zombies? Do I bugger. I'm B Smith. This is my turf. Any zombies on the loose should be worried about *me*!

FIVE

That night I have the nightmare again. I've been tormented by it for as long as I can remember. Always the same and always terrifying.

I'm on a plane. We haven't taken off yet. I'm by the window, but I don't look out. In the dream I never look out.

There's a woman next to me and a baby in the aisle seat. The baby's sitting alone, strapped in by a normal belt. I know that's not right – they have special straps for babies on planes – but in the dream it doesn't seem strange.

The woman's chatting to her child, cooing, making nonsense noises. The baby blanks her. It's staring straight ahead. I don't know if it's a boy or a girl—it's dressed in white clothes.

We taxi down the runway. The engine roars. The plane tears free of the ground and whines like a dying dog. I shake in my seat. My stomach clenches. I don't mind flying, but I hate take-off. We go abroad most years, Costa del Sol, Cyprus, Ibiza. Each time we rise, I'm sure that the engine will stall, that the plane will drop sickeningly, that I'll die from an explosion or burn to death slowly. The fear passes when we level out, but for that first minute or two . . . absolute terror.

It's no different in the dream. Except in a way it is. Because I know something worse than a crash is coming. I sense it in the air. The roar of a plane engine is always menacing, but this sounds worse. It sounds *hungry*.

The woman starts to cry. She doesn't raise her hands, just sits upright, sobbing, tears streaming down her cheeks. I stare at her, wanting to say something, but struck dumb by fear of what's to come.

Then the baby speaks.

'*don't cry mummy.*'

Its voice is tinny, barely a whisper, but it carries above the roar of the engine. The woman doesn't look at the baby or stop crying.

'*don't be frightened mummy*,' the baby says. '*we're with you. we'll always be with you.*'

The baby's head turns. But it's not looking at its mother. It's looking at me. It has no pupils, just balls of white for eyes.

'*you're yummy mummy*,' the baby whispers. It should be funny but it isn't. The unnatural infant has a full set of teeth, all sharpened into fangs. Drops of blood drip from the sides of its mouth as it speaks.

The baby stands. (I don't know what happened to the belt.) I stare at it and it stares at me. The woman between us has vanished. The baby looks like a doll, not moving, not breathing, white eyes, sharp teeth, blood.

'*don't be frightened mummy*,' the baby says. Except its lips don't move. After a confused moment I realise the voice came from the seat in front. I tear my gaze away from the baby and look ahead.

Another baby is clinging to the top of the seat. I can see its face and shoulders, its perfect, tiny hands. It has the same type of clothes as the baby next to me. Same white eyes and sharp teeth. But no blood on this one's lips. Not yet.

'*we'll save you mummy*,' the baby in front whispers.

'*we'll always be with you mummy.*' Another voice, from behind.

The baby in my row is in the seat next to me now. The top of its head doesn't quite reach my chin. It's leaning forward. I should be able to knock it away with a single swipe. But I don't move. I can't.

'*you have to die now mummy,*' the baby says, and '*die*' is echoed in whispers around the cabin.

I half-rise and look over the top of the seats ahead of me. Babies everywhere, all standing, climbing the seats, looking at me, whispering '*die*'.

I glance back—more of the same. Scores of babies clambering over the seats, but calmly, smoothly, faces blank, eyes white, mouths open, teeth flashing.

I cringe away from the monstrous babies and press hard against the window. I think I'm crying, but I can't be sure. The babies crawl over the seats, closer and closer, a tide of them, all looking the same. Only their fingers move, little flickers of flesh and bone. Otherwise they could be gliding.

The baby next to me climbs into my lap and stands, feet planted on my thighs, face right in front of mine now. Others crowd round it. Unnaturally slender fingers fasten on my legs, my ankles, my wrists, my arms. A baby grabs my ears and pulls back my head, exposing my throat. There are more babies on the ceiling, hanging from it like angels or vampires.

'*join us mummy,*' the baby directly in front of me says. The blood on its chin has dried. It falls off in flaky scabs.

'*die mummy,*' the others croon.

'*you're one of us,*' the baby in my lap snarls, and suddenly its face changes. Its eyes glare red. Its lips contort into a sneer. Lines of hatred warp its clammy flesh. '*you're one of us mummy,*' it shrieks.

The baby thrusts forward and latches onto my throat. Those clinging to the ceiling drop. The rest press in around me. All of their mouths are open, rows of tiny, shiny teeth. All make a sickening moaning sound.

Then they bite . . .

SIX

... and I wake up.

I'm shaking and sweating. I always am after the nightmare. I feel like I've been screaming, but in all these years I've never made a sound. Mum and Dad would have told me if I had.

I only wear underpants and a T-shirt to bed. I used to wear pyjamas, but I'd always sweat through them when I had the dream and have to dump them the next day.

I get up and stagger to the bathroom. I take off the T-shirt on the way and drop it by the foot of my bed, knowing Mum will stick it in the laundry basket in the morning.

I sit on the toilet, shivering. I don't need to pee. I just

have to wait somewhere outside my bedroom for a bit, until the shakes pass.

I hate that bloody dream. Apart from when Dad is on the rampage, it's the only time I ever feel truly scared, lost, out of my depth, helpless. What's worse, I can't tell anyone about it. What would it look like, someone my age admitting they're scared by a dream about babies? I mean, if it was cannibals or monsters or something, fair enough. But bloody *babies*!

Dad would skin me if he heard I still have the nightmare. When I'd go crying to him as a kid, he'd tell me not to be stupid, there was nothing scary about babies. When I kept bothering him, he whipped me with his belt. He asked a few weeks later if I was still having the dream. I forced a grin and said I wasn't.

When the shakes stop, I get up and wash my face and hands. I wipe sweat from my back with a towel, then pause and study myself in the mirror. My eyes are bloodshot and blurry with traces of fear – I think I sometimes cry quietly in my sleep – so I splash water over them and rub them with my knuckles until it hurts. Next time I check, I just look angry. That's better.

I study my light blue eyes and admire my stubbled head. Flex my biceps. Rub a faded yellow bruise on my left arm where Dad thumped me a week ago when I didn't hand him the remote quick enough. I wink at myself and mutter, 'Looking good, B.'

I massage my stomach, to loosen the tightened muscles, then pick at the faded white scar near the top of my right thigh. It's a small c shape, from an injection I had when I was two or three years old. It was a new type of flu vaccine. Dad volunteered me for it—they were paying good money for guinea pigs. Mum was worried, but Dad said there was no way they'd test it on babies if there was any chance it would cause harm.

He was right and it worked a treat. I've never even had a cold. I don't know why it didn't make it to the shops. Maybe there were side-effects and I'm one of the lucky ones who didn't suffer any. Or maybe they have to wait a certain amount of time before they can put it on the market.

I scowl and stop picking the c scar. The things that go through your mind at – I check my watch – 3:27 in the morning. I should be sleeping, not analysing a dumb bloody scar. I grin at myself. 'You're a stupid . . .'

I stop. In the mirror I spot a baby standing on the laundry basket, hands red with blood, eyes white, teeth glinting. It breathes out and a small cloud of red mist rises from its mouth.

I shut my eyes and count to five, taking quick breaths, cursing myself for my weakness. When I look again, there's nobody behind me.

I stomp from the bathroom and back to bed. I grab a fresh T-shirt from my wardrobe and glare as I pull it on, mad at myself for letting the nightmare freak me out so much.

'It was only a dream, B,' I whisper as I lie beneath the covers, eyes wide, knowing I won't get a wink of sleep again tonight. 'Only a dream. Only a dream. Only a …'

SEVEN

School. Tired and grumpy. I hate the nightmare more than ever. I'm a teenager. I should be dreaming about getting hot and steamy with movie stars, not about killer babies. I was sure I'd leave the dream behind as I got older, but no such luck. I still have it two or three nights a week.

I barely listen in class at the best of times. Today I tune out completely and scribble crude drawings over my books. I suck at art, but I like to doodle when I'm bored.

Most of my teachers ignore me. They know I'm a lost cause and they don't try to reach out to me. They also know I'm not someone you mess with. One of them crossed me a couple of years ago. I'd been in a fight and had been summoned to the principal's office. The teacher saw me waiting outside and whispered something to one of his colleagues. Both men sniggered. Then he said out loud, 'But what can you expect from someone with a father like *that*?'

Someone punctured the tyres on that teacher's car. Someone found out where he lived and threw a brick through his window. Someone stuck up pictures of him around the local area with his phone number and the message, *Ring for a good time!*

I'm not saying who that someone was, but when he came creeping up to B Smith in school one day and meekly said, 'Sorry for what I said about your dad,' he was left in peace after that.

I fall asleep in history. Jonesenzio is duller than most of our teachers. I'm not the only one to snooze in his class.

'Fire!' someone hisses in my ear and I jolt awake, almost falling off my chair.

Meths and Kray laugh their faces off as Jonesenzio scowls at me.

'Sods,' I spit at them, rubbing my elbow where I hit it on the desk.

'If you're *quite* finished . . .' Jonesenzio murmurs.

'Sorry, Mr Jones,' I simper. 'I thought I saw a mouse.'

He drones on. I don't mind Jonesenzio. He's given me a C on every essay we've been assigned for the last three years, even though I've never handed one in.

Mum sometimes grouches about my lousy grades. 'How come you can't do well in the other subjects, like you do in history?' Dad tosses me a wink when she goes on like that. He had Jonesenzio when he was younger. He knows the score.

'I bet you were dreaming about me,' Meths chuckles, keeping his voice low so as not to disturb the teacher. Jonesenzio doesn't complain if you talk loudly in his class, but he stops talking and stands there silently, look-ing at you politely, which is even worse. A couple of us tested him once and found that he's happy to do that for an entire class. You'll never out-patient the Jones.

'Yeah,' I tell Meths. 'It was a real nightmare.'

Meths is the biggest guy in our year and the oldest. He started school a year later than most of us and has been held back twice. That's where he got his nickname, short for Methuselah. I wish I could lay claim to that, but it wasn't one of mine. I'd no idea who Methuselah was until someone explained it to me.

'You can copy my notes later,' Kray says seriously.

'Notes?' I take the bait.

He holds up a drawing. Kray's a much better artist than me. The picture is of La Lips, naked, being given some after-school tuition by a very animated Jonesenzio.

I smother a laugh and raise my knuckles for him to knock. 'Don't let Copper see it,' I gasp.

'I was hoping he could correct any anatomical inaccuracies,' Kray says.

'Like you haven't seen La Lips in the swimming pool,' Meths snorts and this time we all have to smother laughs. It's an old story that La Lips shows everything in the public pool if you give her a quid. No truth in it as far as I know, but when did that ever stop a good story?

History ends (if only!) and we roll out into the yard for lunch. I scoff a bag of crisps and nick a bar of chocolate from a girl in a lower year. She tries to fight me for it, but her friends pull her off. I sneer as they haul her away. She had a narrow escape. In my current mood I'd have happily taken her into the toilet and half-drowned her. If her friends hadn't pulled her clear when they did . . .

I spend most of the break with Meths, Kray, Trev, Ballydefeck, Suze, La Lips, Copper, Dunglop and Elephant. The usual gang, except for Linzer and Pox, who are off somewhere else.

There's a new zombie clip circulating on the internet. Copper shows it to us on his phone. It's footage of an undead soldier. If the clip is genuine, it looks like he was one of the team sent in to eliminate the Pallaskenry mob. He must have been infected, got away, tangled with some humans later.

In the clip, several men are pounding the zombie with shovels and axes. One of them strikes his left arm a few times and it tears loose. Another of the men picks it up and starts whacking the zombie over the head with it, cheered on by his team.

I laugh the first time I watch the clip. Most of the others do too. It's comical, a guy being slapped around with his own severed arm.

Then, as Copper replays it a couple of times, I start focusing on the finer details. The terror in the men's eyes. The rage and hunger in the soldier's. The flecks of dried blood around his mouth, a sign that he must have fed prior to his run-in with the vigilantes. The long bits of bone sticking out of his fingers. His fangs.

The clip stops with the guys hitting the zombie, leaving us to guess how it ends. I imagine one of the group chopping off the soldier's head with an axe, the men pulping it beneath their feet, not stopping until every last scrap of brain has been mulched. That's how they kill zombies in films, by destroying their brains. Does that work in real life too? I assume so but I'm not sure.

There's silence when Copper turns off his phone. We're all troubled by what we've seen. We can't even make a joke about it. Not yet. It feels too real at the moment. We need time to absorb and then dismiss it.

Elephant starts rabbiting on about football in order to break the solemn mood. He's a real fanatic, goes to matches all the time. I watch the highlights on TV most weeks, so that I can discuss the goals with the others, but football bores me.

Elephant finishes moaning about the weekend's match and pauses for breath.

'Enough already,' I snap. 'You're doing my head in.'

'Who rattled your cage?' Elephant scowls.

'You did,' I tell him. 'And if you don't shut it, I'll cut you down to size.'

Lots of catcalls, everyone relieved to have something else to think about, welcoming the distraction. Elephant didn't get his nickname because he's tall or fat, but because of what his mates saw the first time he undressed for a shower after gym.

'Leave my trunk alone,' Elephant smirks, crossing his hands protectively in front of himself.

'Are you all right?' Trev asks me. 'You're like a tiger today.'

'Knackered,' I growl. 'Didn't get much sleep.'

'Worried about zombies?' Suze asks sympathetically.

'Don't be daft,' I tell her. 'I'm dreading the exams.'

Everyone laughs, forgetting about the clip, putting it behind us, slipping back into our normal routines as if we'd never been disturbed.

'You won't get into Oxford if you don't get straight As,' Dunglop says.

'I prefer Cambridge anyway,' I sniff.

'God, imagine if you *did* get in,' Meths says and we stare at him. 'I mean on a sports scholarship or something.'

'You ever see me playing any sports?' I jeer.

'No, but maybe there's some other ...' Meths pulls a face and tries to remember what he wanted to say. I fail classes because I don't give a damn. Meths, bless him, really *is* thick.

The bell rings and I slap Meths' back. 'Come on. I don't think either of us has to worry about Cambridge or Oxford. I'll be amazed if we make it out of this place.'

'Yeah, but . . .' Meths shrugs and smiles, letting go of whatever crazy thought it was that he had. Thoughts never stick long with Meths. If zombies ever do attack, he has nothing to worry about. With that tiny brain, he's the last one they'll target!

EIGHT

Biology. One of the few classes where I pay attention. Not because I'm fascinated by the digestive system of the worm (give me strength!) but because I like the teacher, Mr Burke.

Burke impressed me the first day he walked into class and said, 'I know most of you couldn't give a toss about biology, but if you don't give me any grief, I'll do my best to make it interesting for you.'

Burke's the best of our teachers, maybe the only really good one that we have. I don't know what he's doing in this dump. He should be at a private school like the one Vinyl moved to. He's wasted here, stuck with mugs like Meths and Kray and ... yeah, I can admit it ... me.

Dad doesn't share my high opinion of Mr Burke and has tried a few times to have him drummed out, or at least confined to teaching kids of his own race. Which is odd, because the lightly coloured Burke is of a mixed background. I would have thought that meant he could claim membership of either side, but Dad doesn't see it that way. He moans about Burke all the time and I nod like the obedient little puppy that I am and simper, 'Yes, Dad. No, Dad. Three bags full, Dad.' It sickens me but what can I do? If I told him Burke's a cool teacher, he'd hammer me. Easier to say nothing and keep my head down.

Burke is trying hard to make the dissection of a worm seem like an earth-shattering event, but it's hard to keep us interested in crap like this. After a while Trev puts up a hand. 'Sir?'

'Go on,' Burke sighs, looking up from the worm with an expression that seems to suggest he finds this particular lesson as boring as the rest of us.

'Can we dissect a zombie next, sir?'

Laughter.

'If you bring me one, I'll certainly help you cut it up,' Burke says drily, then pushes the worm aside. I grin at Trev and give him a cheesy thumbs up. It's great when we sidetrack Burke. He doesn't let it happen often – he insists on covering the course inside out – but every now and then he'll relent.

'Who believes that zombies are real?' Burke asks.

A few hands go up but not many. It's not that we don't believe, just that we don't want to be seen to be enthusiastic in class.

'Come on,' Burke snaps. 'A real show of hands or it's back to the worm.'

We groan, then hands start creeping up. Soon most of them are in the air.

Burke does a slow count, then says softly, 'Why?'

We gawp at him.

'Why?' he says again. 'Because they're on TV? Because you've seen photos and video clips?'

'Yeah,' someone says.

'But they can do anything with digital equipment these days, can't they?' he smirks.

'Don't you believe, sir?' I ask. I was one of the few to keep their hand down.

'Actually I do,' he says. 'But let's explore alternatives.' He turns to the whiteboard, grabs a pen and writes *Media hoax? Publicity for a film or TV show?* Looks over his shoulder at us. 'Any other ideas?'

'It's a conspiracy,' Stagger Lee snorts.

'The government?' Burke asks.

'Yeah.'

'The Irish? Ours? America's?'

Stagger Lee shrugs. 'The whole bloody lot.'

'What for?' Burke asks. 'Why go to all that trouble?'

Silence for a moment, then Linzer – one of the smartest in our year – puts up her hand and says, 'Experiment gone wrong.'

'Good,' Burke beams and adds it to the whiteboard. 'What sort of experiment?'

'Chemical weapons,' Linzer says. 'Maybe they were testing something and it accidentally got into the water or air. Or they released it on purpose.'

'Which is more likely?' Burke asks, nodding at Elephant.

'Dunno,' Elephant says.

'B?'

'A test,' I say confidently.

'Why?' he presses.

'Pallaskenry's in the middle of nowhere. They wouldn't have any labs around there. It's all bogland.'

'Excellent, B.'

I find myself grinning goofily. Nobody has a dig at me to bring me down to size either, like they would if this was any other class.

'More ideas,' Burke says, pointing to Suze.

'God, I don't know.' She blushes, then coughs. 'My dad thinks it's terrorists.'

Burke blinks. 'Come again?'

'He thinks the army went in looking for terrorists. Got carried away and killed civilians by mistake. Then cooked up this zombie story to give them an excuse to kill the witnesses.'

'Far-fetched,' Burke hums, 'but let's run with it.' He adds the theory to the board and asks for more suggestions.

Someone thinks the zombies are robots gone wild. Another says maybe it's aliens, that the rabid crazies were taken over by bodiless beings from another planet. Kray comes up with a twist on the experiment angle, only he figures people are being controlled by satellite signals.

'They're gonna use it on the Arabs,' he says. 'No more sending our troops in to sort out their messes. Drive the buggers mad and leave them to it. They'll wipe them-selves out and good riddance to them.'

The Muslim kids don't like that. Angry mutterings. Burke shushes them.

'That's not one of the more far-fetched ideas,' he says. 'Certain politicians would do just about anything to cling to power and disable our enemies. Kray was insulting – grow up and stop acting like a thug – but he might have a point.'

'I don't think it's terrifying,' I snort, evil-eyeing the Muslims. 'In fact I hope Kray's right, that we *are* going after them. They'd do it to us if they could.'

'We'll have that argument another day,' Burke barks, stopping a war before it can erupt. 'Let's stick to zombies. Any other proposals?'

There are a few more, then Burke stands back to study what he's written. 'It's a horrible world, isn't it?' he mutters and I'm not sure he knows that he's spoken out loud.

He turns to us. 'I'm not saying I believe any of these exotic, foundless theories. But these are questions we should be asking. Life's complicated. Answers rarely come wrapped up nice and simple. There are plenty of people out there ready to tell us what we should and shouldn't believe. We always need to be sceptical, to look for the sting in the tale.'

Burke looks around slowly and it seems like he's staring at each and every one of us in turn. 'Trust no one. Always question what you're told. Don't believe the lies that people feed you, even if they're your teachers or parents. At the end of the day you have to work out for yourself what's right or wrong.'

He glances back at the board and sighs. 'But bear this in mind. There are lots of black-hearted, mean-spirited bastards in the world.' There are some gasps when he swears but most of us take no notice. 'It's important that we hold them to account. But always remember that *you* might be the most black-hearted and mean-spirited of the lot, so hold yourself the most accountable of all.'

As we try to make sense of that, Burke chuckles, shakes his head and wipes the board clean. 'Enough preaching,' he says brightly, then adds, to a chorus of groans, 'Back to the worm . . .'

NINE

The last class ends and we churn out, shouting,
laughing, swearing. Normally I can't escape the building quick enough, but today I head deeper into it.
There's a five-a-side football tournament in the gym.
I'm not playing, and I'm not really bothered about
watching, but it'll be more fun than hanging out on the
streets.

Kray, Elephant, Trev, Linzer and I wind our way
through the labyrinth of corridors. Our school's massive. It holds over a thousand students and it used to be
even bigger. It wasn't always the cesspit it is now. Once
upon a time they sank money into this place, kept
adding on new rooms. It's not very wide but it's deep.

Takes several minutes, with all the twists and turns, to get from one end to the other.

No outdoor spaces apart from a few small courtyards. The gym's a huge room at the rear of the building, solid walls all round, a few narrow skylight windows high overhead, lots of artificial light. The phys-ed staff keep it in good nick. You can play football, basketball, hockey, badminton. They have foosball and pool tables stacked at the sides—they bring them out at lunch for those who are so easily amused.

We hit the gym and spread out. There's already a crowd and the first game has kicked off. The teams are from the year above ours, so we give them loads of abuse, trying to distract them. One player shoots us the finger and we cheer.

'Bloody idiots,' I laugh. 'Running around like maniacs.'

'It's the beautiful game,' Elephant argues. He loves football, but hasn't played in ages, still recovering from breaking his foot a few months back.

'Beautiful waste of time,' I tease him, but he's too engrossed in the game to pay me much attention.

I get bored quickly and look around for something else to do. There's a small group to our left, cheering on the players, a mix of kids from different years. I don't know most of them, but one catches my eye—Tyler Bayor.

My dad had a bust-up with Tyler's old man a while back. Tyler's dad had accused me of stealing from his son. It was true – I took money from him a few times, like I took the bar of chocolate from the girl today, because Tyler's soft and the cash was there for the taking – but I denied it until I was blue in the face.

My dad was furious that a black guy had dared point the finger at me. Marched round to their home, dragged Tyler's dad outside, fought with him in the street. Others separated them before it got nasty. We retreated with our heads held high and Tyler's dad didn't push the charges any further.

I stopped stealing from Tyler, even though Dad told me he didn't care what I did to *that walking fart of a kid*. I didn't stop because I'd been challenged. I stopped because I knew Dad thought that I was targeting Tyler because of his colour. I wasn't. I picked on Tyler because he was weak and I could get away with it. But I felt uneasy, seeing myself through my dad's eyes, like I was the same as him.

I never told any of the others about what happened, which is why Vinyl didn't realise it was personal when I was having a go at Tyler in the park. I'm not sure why

I kept it secret. I guess I was ashamed, not of stealing, but of my dad turning it into a racial thing.

Even though I don't steal from Tyler any more, I don't like him. The sight of him reminds me of that night, my dad squaring up to Tyler's old man, me feeling proud and mortified at the same time, all of it brought on by Tyler not keeping his mouth shut and putting up with the theft as any good victim should.

'Hey, Tyler,' I shout. 'Why didn't you come play with us the other night?'

Tyler looks at me and forces a laugh. Turns back to the game, hoping I'll let it drop. But I'm not in the dropping mood.

'Oi! Don't ignore me.'

'I'm not ignoring you, B,' he sighs.

'You bloody are.'

The kids around him back away and focus on the game. None of them wants to get sucked into this.

Tyler gulps and faces me. 'I was looking for a mate. He wasn't there. So I left.'

'But you didn't even stop to say hello,' I remind him.

'That was rude,' Kray chuckles, giving me a dig in the ribs, egging me on.

'I know your kind aren't the most civilised in the

world,' I continue, taking a few steps towards the small, nervous kid, 'but I thought you'd have the good manners to —'

'What do you mean *your kind*?' someone snaps.

I halt and blink. A tall black girl has stepped forward. She's glaring at me. She's from the year above mine, Nancy something-or-other.

'You got a problem?' I snarl.

'Yeah,' she says, stepping in front of Tyler, who can't believe his luck. 'You just said that blacks are uncivilised.'

'Not me,' I grin.

'Yes, you did,' she huffs. 'I heard what you said. *Your kind.*'

'Maybe I was talking about his family,' I chuckle. 'Or the fans of the team he supports.'

'No,' Nancy says. 'I know exactly what you meant.'

I shrug and fake a yawn. Nancy's got me dead to rights, but I can't admit that in front of the others. It's not in my nature to back down. You can never show weakness. You have to fight every fight that comes your way. Otherwise you end up being picked on like Tyler.

'Let's say you're right,' I drawl. 'So what?'

'I won't stand for racism,' Nancy says. 'Apologise or I'll report you.'

'Me?' I gasp. 'Racist? You're loop the loop. Isn't she, Kray?'

Kray chuckles weakly, but says nothing. He doesn't want the hassle.

'Tell her I'm not a racist, Tyler. Tell her you and me are good friends and were just having a laugh.'

'Leave him alone,' Nancy says. 'Pick on me if you want to pick on someone.'

I grin tightly. 'All right.' I move closer and get in her face, even though I have to go right up on my toes. 'I *was* talking about blacks,' I murmur. I know it's madness, that I won't be able to justify this if she grasses me up. But I've only two choices here—apologise or push through with the hard-nosed, racist routine. And I wasn't brought up to apologise. Certainly not to the likes of her.

Nancy pushes me away. 'You're scum,' she sneers.

'At least I'm white scum,' I toss back at her, slipping into hateful character with alarming ease.

'You'll be suspended scum once I tell a teacher what you said.'

'Is that how you deal with people who wind you up?' I jeer. 'You run to the teachers?'

'Yeah.'

I shrug. 'Go on then. It's my word against yours. But while you're complaining about me, I'll complain too.

You pushed me. That's physical assault and everyone saw it.'

'Rubbish,' she snorts.

'You raised your hands and pushed me. That's a direct attack.'

I step up close to Nancy and smile. 'If you're gonna get done just for pushing me, you might as well go the whole hog. Go on, knock my block off, you know you want to. You lot love to fight, don't you? It's what you were born for. Well, that and basketball.'

Nancy's fingers bunch into fists. She's trembling. She wants to hit me, but she'll lose the moral high ground if she does. If she strikes the first blow, she won't be able to turn me in. It doesn't matter if you're provoked—school policy is that you should never react.

'Go on,' I whisper, then sink lower than I ever thought I would, and make a few soft, gorilla-like grunting noises.

Nancy shrieks and slaps me. I laugh.

'Is that the hardest you can hit?' I mock her.

She slaps me again, a flurry of feeble blows. I don't even bother to raise my hands to protect myself. 'Help me!' I yell theatrically. 'She's gone mad. I think she has rabies. Don't let her bite. I'm afraid she'll –'

One of Nancy's rings catches my cheek and tears into it. I hiss and slap her away. A thin trickle of blood flows from the cut. The sight of it goads Nancy on. She throws herself at me and grapples for my eyes with her nails, kicking my shins, screaming shrilly. I put a hand on her face to push her away. She bites my fingers.

I grit my teeth and tear my hand free. Nancy goes for my eyes again. Losing my temper, I step back and let fly, a real punch. My fist hits the side of her face and she goes down. She lands hard and cries out. I start after her to finish her off, but Elephant and Kray get in my way.

'Easy, B,' Kray says. 'She's not as tough as you.'

'I don't care,' I shout. 'She bit me. I'm gonna –'

'B Smith!' someone roars.

I look up and groan. It's Stuttering Stan, one of the PE teachers. He doesn't really stutter, but he trips over his tongue sometimes.

'You're in for it now,' Nancy cackles, smiling through her tears of pain and anger.

'You hit me first,' I snarl.

'Tell it to Stuttering Stan,' she crows.

I spit at her as if I was a child, then turn and stand to attention, staring directly at Stuttering Stan as he strides towards me, acting as if I've done nothing wrong. I know I should feel ashamed of myself, and to a degree I do. But to my surprise and dismay, I also feel smug, because I know Dad would be proud if he could see me now, bringing an interfering black girl down a peg or two.

TEN

Stuttering Stan takes me to the principal's office. Very neat, everything in its place. A shining computer in one corner. Diplomas on the walls. A small plaque on her desk, *Mrs Lynne Reed, Principal*, just in case anyone is in any doubt.

Nancy's already outside, waiting her turn. I'm sitting across from Mrs Reed, gaze glued to the floor, waiting for her to start in on me. She transferred here the year that I started, and I was one of the first students she had to discipline, just a couple of days into her new job. I've had to explain myself to her a lot of times since then, though in my defence it's been a while since I was last hauled before her.

Mrs Reed flicks through a file, slowly. I'm guessing it's about me. I try not to fidget. My face is red and I keep my hands tucked under my legs, in case she spots them trembling. I shouldn't be worried. I'm in trouble, sure, but Dad won't give me any grief, not when he hears what it was about. Still, I'm in the wrong and Mrs Reed isn't the sort of person who makes you feel at ease in a situation like this. She looks like something from an ancient movie, black cape, silver hair, thin-rimmed glasses.

'I don't like it when my students fight,' she finally says, putting the file aside.

'Nancy started it,' I say evenly, careful not to sound like I'm whining.

'I'll let Miss Price state her case once I'm through with you,' Mrs Reed says. 'I suspect her story will differ significantly from yours. Please tell me what happened, and try to be honest if you can.'

I was going to spin it, but that last line stings me. It's like she's challenging me. So I decide to hit her with the facts. If I'm going down, I might as well go down with my dignity intact, not whimpering and making up stories.

'I was having a dig at Tyler.'

'Tyler Bayor?' she asks.

'Yeah. Nancy stuck her nose in and told me I was being racist.'

'Were you?'

'No.' I scowl. 'I mean, yeah, in a way I was, but nothing bad. I said something about his kind not being civilised.'

'That was stupid,' Mrs Reed murmurs.

I bristle but don't retort. Because she's right—it *was* stupid.

'Anyway,' I mutter, 'Nancy squared up to me. I told her to butt out. She didn't. Then she slapped me.'

'She struck first?' Mrs Reed asks.

'Yeah. Everyone saw her.'

'And you hit back?'

'No. I let her slap me a few times. I tried to make a joke out of it. But then she cut me and I lost my rag.'

'I see. Is there anything else you wish to add?'

I think about stopping there, but Mrs Reed is looking at me archly, like she still doesn't think I'm capable of telling the truth. 'I made some gorilla noises,' I sigh, my blush deepening.

Mrs Reed hums, picks up my file again and glances through it.

'I know your father,' she says out of the blue.

'My dad?' I frown.

'Yes,' she says. 'We share concerns about our nation's disintegrating morals and have attended many of the same meetings over the years.'

I blink, confusion turning into outright bewilderment. Dad has never talked about Mrs Reed. I can't imagine where they could have run into one another, except at parent-teacher evenings.

'Your father is an upstanding member of the community,' Mrs Reed continues, and I have to choke back a scornful laugh. 'He works tirelessly for the things he believes in. Always there to lend his support when it is needed, giving selflessly of his time and energy. We need people like him. People like *you*. People who want to make Britain great again, who are prepared to fly in the face of public apathy and political correctness.'

She pauses to make sure I'm on her wavelength. And I am. Mrs Reed must share Dad's low opinion of foreigners. I wouldn't have thought someone in her position could be as small-minded and bigoted as my old man, but thinking back to the meetings he's made me attend, there were all sorts present. I guess racists come from every walk of life.

'This is not where we fight our battles,' Mrs Reed says as I gawp at her. 'You achieve nothing by stirring up trouble like this. You merely hand ammunition to those who wish to undermine our cause. When you get into difficulties of this nature, it reflects poorly on your father, and by extension on the rest of us.'

'I wasn't fighting any battles,' I wheeze. 'I was just having a go at Tyler and then Nancy got in my way and . . .'

Mrs Reed smiles gently. 'I know it can be frustrating when people like Nancy interfere. Like your father, I am critical of this government's immigration policies. They have let in too many people of Nancy's calibre, and afforded them far too prominent a voice. But we must fight sensibly for a sensible Britain. When you are older, you can vote and campaign and express your concerns politically. The tide is turning. Public opinion is swinging our way, and will continue to do so, but only if people can trust us, if we behave calmly and responsibly. We must rise above insults and petty fights. We're better than that.

'You can return to class now,' Mrs Reed says. 'I'll have a talk with Miss Price. Since she slapped you first, I'm sure I'll be able to convince her to let the matter drop. But, to be safe, tomorrow I want you to take her to one side and apologise.'

'But —' I start to object.

'It's that or a suspension,' Mrs Reed snaps.

I fall silent. I wasn't going to argue about the apology. I was going to say that this isn't fair. I thought she was going to chew me a new arsehole. I didn't expect her to sympathise with me. I wasn't fighting for a cause. I'm not like my dad. I don't give a stuff about any of that crap. I expected her to bawl me out, suspend me, maybe expel me. Instead she's commending me. For making gorilla noises to a black girl.

It's wrong. I lost my head and did something I shouldn't have. That was bad but this is worse. It's disturbing to think that a woman in Mrs Reed's position would praise me for losing my temper and saying such a thing.

But how dumb would I need to be to criticise my principal for being a racist? She's giving me a get-out-of-jail-free card. I'd have to be a moron or a martyr to turn that down. And I'm neither.

'All right,' I mutter and get up and go.

I don't look at Nancy as I pass. I can't meet her eye. She probably thinks it's because I'm upset at having been punished. But it's not. It's because I'm ashamed that Mrs Reed thinks I'm a racist. And because I'm worried that she might be right.

ELEVEN

On my way home, I choose to tell Dad about what happened with Tyler, Nancy and Mrs Reed, figuring it's better he hear about it from me than someone else.

To my surprise, Dad is already there when I arrive. He must have clocked off early. He's in the kitchen, talking with someone. No sign of Mum.

Dad often has people over to the flat. As Mrs Reed noted, he's heavily involved with local movements to stem the tide of immigration and keep Britain white. He does a lot of canvassing for politicians, works hard behind the scenes, helps stir things up.

I've always tried to stay out of that area of his life, but it's getting harder. Now that I'm older, he's started taking me to meetings. I've been on a few rallies with him too, and once he took me to a house packed with Muslims. I stood outside while he went in and had a long conversation with them. Well, it was more of a screaming match. I could hear them from outside, the Muslims shrieking, Dad shouting even louder. I felt small and afraid, no idea what was going on or what would happen next, standing in the middle of the street like a lemon, wondering what I should do if Dad never reappeared.

But he did emerge in the end, and I saw a Muslim guy glowering behind him. Dad pointed to me and said, 'That's who I fight for—my kid, my wife, my friends. Anything ever happens to any of them, I'll come back here and burn the lot of you down to the ground.'

Then Dad hugged me hard. I glared at the Muslim and shot him the finger. Dad laughed, clapped my back, took me for dinner and bought me the biggest hamburger I'd ever seen. I felt bad about it afterwards, but at the time I was on cloud nine.

Part of me knows I should stop acting, that I'm on thin ice, growing less sure of where the actor ends and the real me begins. When I grunted at Nancy, that wasn't part of an act. That came from the soul.

I should tell Dad I don't share his views, that I'm not warped inside like he is, start standing up to him. But how can you say such a thing to your father? He loves me, I know he does, despite the beatings when he's angry. It would break his heart if I told him what I really thought of him.

Dad doesn't like to be disturbed when he's discussing the state of affairs with his friends and associates, so even though I'm hungry, I slide on by the kitchen, planning to head straight to my room. But Dad must hear me because he calls out, 'B? Is that you?'

'Yeah.'

'Come here a minute.'

He sounds more subdued than usual. That tips me off to the fact that there might be somebody important with him. Dad's loud and bullish most of the time, but quiet and submissive around people he respects.

I head into the kitchen, expecting someone in a suit with a politically perfect smile. But I stagger to a halt halfway through the door and stare uncertainly. The guy with Dad is like nobody I've ever seen before.

The man is standing by the table, sipping from a cup of coffee. He sets it down when he spots me and arches an eyebrow, amused by my reaction.

He's very tall, maybe six foot six, and thin, except for

a large potbelly. It looks weird on such a slender frame, and the buttons on the pink shirt he's wearing beneath his striped jacket strain to hold it in. He has a mop of white hair and pale skin. Not albino pale, but damn close. Long, creepy-looking fingers.

But it's his eyes which prove so startling. They're by far the biggest I've ever seen, at least twice the size of mine. Almost totally white, except for a dark, tiny pupil at the centre of each. As soon as I see him, I immediately think, *Owl Man*. I almost say it out loud, but catch myself in time. Dad would hit the roof if I insulted one of his guests.

'So this is the infamous B Smith,' the man chuckles. He has a smooth, cultured voice. He sounds like a radio presenter, but one of the old guys you hear on a Sunday afternoon on the station your gran listens to.

'Yeah,' Dad says. He runs a hand over my head and smiles as if he's in pain and trying to hide it. 'How was school?'

'Fine,' I mutter, unable to tear my gaze away from Owl Man's enormous, cartoonish eyes.

'Some people think it's rude to stare,' Owl Man says jollily, 'but I've always considered it a sign of honest curiosity.'

'Sorry,' I say, blushing at the polite rebuke.

'No need to be,' Owl Man laughs. 'The young *should* be curious, and open too. You should have nothing to hide or apologise for at your tender age. Leave that to decrepit old warhorses like your father and me.'

Dad clears his throat and looks questioningly at Owl Man. 'Anything you'd like to ask?' he says meekly.

'Not just now,' Owl Man purrs and waves a long, bony hand at me. 'You may proceed. It has been nice seeing you again.'

'Again?' I frown, certain I've never met this guy before. There's no way I could have forgotten eyes like that.

'I saw you when you were a child. You were a cute little thing. Sweet enough to eat.'

Owl Man gnashes his teeth playfully, but there's nothing funny about the way he does it and I get goose-bumps up my arms and the back of my neck.

'I'm going to my room,' I tell Dad and hurry out without saying anything else. I half-expect Dad to call me back and bark at me for not saying a proper good-bye, but he lets me go without a word.

I find it hard to settle. I keep thinking about the guy in the kitchen, those unnaturally large eyes. Who the hell is he? He doesn't look like anyone else my dad has ever invited round.

I surf the web for a while, then stick on my headphones and listen to my iPod. I shut my eyes and bop my head to the music, trying to lose myself in the tunes. Sometime later, opening my eyes to stare at the ceiling, I spot Owl Man standing just inside the door to my room.

'Bloody hell!' I shout, ripping off the headphones and sitting up quickly.

'I did knock,' Owl Man says, 'but there was no answer.'

'How long have you been standing there?' I yell, trying to remember if I'd been scratching myself inappropriately over the last five or ten minutes.

'Mere moments,' he says, his smile never slipping.

'Where's my dad?' I ask, heart beating hard. For a crazy second I think that the stranger has killed Dad, maybe pecked him to death, and is now gearing up for an attack on me.

'In the kitchen,' Owl Man says. 'I had to come up to use the facilities.'

He falls silent and stares at me with his big, round eyes. At the back of my mind I hear Mum reading that old fairytale to me when I was younger. *All the better to see you with, my dear.*

'What do you want?' I snap, not caring about

insulting him now, angry at him for invading my privacy.

'I wanted to ask you a question.'

'Oh yeah?' I squint, wondering if he's going to make a pass at me, ready to scream for Dad if he does.

'Do you still have the dream?' he asks and the scream dies silently on my lips.

'What dream?' I croak, but I know the one he means, and he knows that I know. I can see it in his freakish, unsettling eyes.

'The dream about the babies,' Owl Man says softly. 'Your father told me that you had it all the time when you were younger.'

'Why the hell would he tell you something like that?' I try to snap, but it comes out more as a sob.

'I'm interested in dreams,' Owl Man beams. 'Especially dreams of monstrous babies. *mummy*,' he adds in a high-pitched voice, and it sounds just the way the babies in my nightmare say it.

'Get out of my room,' I moan. 'Get out before I call my dad and tell him you tried to molest me.'

'Your father knows I would never do anything like that,' Owl Man sniffs and takes a step closer. 'I'm not leaving until you tell me.'

'No,' I spit. 'I don't have it any more, OK?'

Owl Man studies me silently. Then his lips lift into an even wider, sickening smile. 'You're lying. You *do* still have the dream. How interesting.'

The tall, thin man pats his potbelly, then presses his fingers to his lips and blows me a kiss. 'Good evening, B. It has been a pleasure meeting you again after all these years. Take care of yourself. There are dark times ahead of us. But I think you will fare well.'

With that, he turns and slips out of my room, carefully closing the door behind him. I don't put my headphones back on. I can't move. I just lie on my bed, think about his enormous eyes, wonder at the nature of his questions, and shiver.

TWELVE

I don't see much of Dad over the next few days. It's like he's avoiding me. I want to ask him about the strange visitor, find out his real name, where he's from, why he was here, why Dad told him about my dreams. But Dad clearly doesn't want to discuss it, and what Dad wants, Dad gets.

So I say nothing. I keep my questions to myself. And I try to pretend that my surreal conversation with Owl Man never happened.

On Friday we visit the Imperial War Museum. I've been looking forward to this for weeks and my spirits lift for the first time since my run-in with Nancy and the rest of that bizarre afternoon. We don't go on many school trips—the money isn't there, plus we're buggers to control when we're let loose. Twenty of our lot were taken to the Tate Modern last year and they ran wild. The teachers swore never again, but they seem to have had a change of heart.

'I don't expect you to behave like good little boys and girls,' Burke says on the Tube, to a chorus of jeers and whistles. 'But don't mug me off. I'm in charge of you and I'll be held accountable if you get out of hand. Don't steal, don't beat up the staff and be back at the meeting point at the arranged time.'

'Do we get a prize if we do all that, sir?' Trev asks.

'No,' Burke says. 'You get my respect.'

I love the War Museum. I was here before, when I was in primary school. We were meant to be looking at the World War I stuff, but the tanks and planes in the main hall are what I most remember.

'Look at the bloody cannons!' Elephant gasps as we enter the gardens outside the museum. 'They're massive!'

'You can have a proper look at them later,' Burke says.

'Aw, sir, just a quick look now,' Elephant pleads.

Burke says nothing, just pushes on, and we follow.

The main hall still impresses. I thought it might be disappointing this time, but the tanks and planes are as cool as ever. The planes hang from the ceiling, loads of them, and the ceiling's three or four floors high. Everyone coos, necks craned, then we hurry to the tanks. They're amazing, and you can even crawl into some and pretend that you're driving them. We should be too old for that sort of stuff, but it's like we slip back to when we were ten years old—the lure of the tanks is impossible to resist.

Burke gives us a few minutes to mess around. We're the second group from the school to arrive. As the third lot trickle in, we form a posse and head upstairs to where the Holocaust exhibition starts.

This is the reason we're here. We haven't focused much on the Holocaust in class – at least not that I remember, though I guess I could have slept through it – but our teachers reckon this is important, so they've brought us anyway, regardless of the very real risk that we might start a riot and wreck the place.

Burke stops us just before we go in and makes sure we're all together.

Kray sniffs the air and pulls a face. 'Something's burning.'

I expect Burke to have a go at him, but to my shock it's Jonesenzio – I didn't even know he was here – who speaks up.

'One of my uncles was Polish. He was sent to Auschwitz in the 1930s. Not the death camp, where they gassed people, but the concentration camp. He was worked like a slave until he was a skeleton. Starved. Tortured. The bones in one of his feet were smashed with a hammer. He survived for a long time, longer than most. But in the end he was hung for allegedly stealing food from a guard. They let him hang for nearly ten minutes, without killing him. Then they took him down, let him recover, and hung him again until he was dead.'

Jonesenzio steps up to Kray, stares at him until he looks away, then says softly but loud enough for everyone to hear, 'If there are any more jokes, or if you take one step out of line from this point on, you'll have to answer to *me*.'

It should be funny – pitiful even – but it isn't. Everyone shuts up, and for the first time that I can ever remember, we stay shut up.

The exhibition is horrible. It's not so bad at the start, a bit boring even, where we learn about the build-up to war, how the Nazis came to power, why nobody liked the Jews. But it soon becomes a nightmare as we dip further into the world of ghettos, death camps and gas chambers.

Old film footage of Jews being rounded up and

chased by Nazis hits hard. So does the funeral cart on which piles of corpses were wheeled to mass graves. And the rows of shoes and glasses, taken from people before they were gassed and cremated.

But what unsettles me most is a small book. It belonged to a girl, my sort of age. She wrote stories in it and drew sweet, colourful pictures. As I stare at it, I think, that could have been me. Sitting in my room, writing and drawing. Then dragged out, shipped off to a death camp in a train, shaved bare, stripped naked, gassed, cremated or buried in an unmarked grave with a load of strangers. And all that's left of me is a stupid book I used to scribble in, in a cold, empty room where no one lives any more.

Some of the others cry as we walk through the chambers of atrocity. I don't. But I feel my throat tighten and I have to look away more than once and blink until I'm sure my eyes are going to stay dry.

Coming out of the exhibition is like emerging into sunlight after being in a dark tunnel. The museum doesn't look so much like an adventure park now. The planes and tanks, the cannons, guns and swords which lie scattered around the place . . . They were used to kill people. Not actors, like in the movies. But real people like me and my mum. Like that little girl.

'Sobering stuff, isn't it?' Burke says to a few of us standing silently nearby.

'They were monsters,' I growl.

Burke raises an eyebrow. 'You think so?'

'Nobody human could have done that.'

Burke shrugs, then leans in and whispers so that only I can hear, 'Maybe that's what we should do with the immigrants.'

I gasp and draw back from him, shocked.

Burke raises an eyebrow. 'You look surprised.'

'You can't say things like that!' I protest.

'Why not?' As I stare at him, he says, 'I heard about your fight with Nancy and how Mrs Reed *white* washed it because of her friendship with your father.'

'How do you know about that?' I growl.

'It's no big secret,' he says. 'Aren't the gas chambers where it will all end if Mrs Reed and your father get their way?'

'No!' I shout, then lower my voice when the others look at me strangely. 'How can you even suggest that?'

'Because it's true,' he snaps. 'This is where hatred and intolerance lead. Don't be a child, B, and don't act like you're naive.'

'You're wrong, they just want a society where –'

'Don't,' Burke stops me. 'I've heard all the arguments

before. I'm not going to tell you which side you should be on. You're old enough to choose. All I'm saying is be aware. Know what you're signing up for and accept the consequences. Mrs Reed and your dad are modern-day fascists. Only a fool would think otherwise.'

Then he walks off and leaves me trembling.

I think about the Nazis. I think about my dad.

'It's not true,' I whisper. 'They're not the same.'

But a voice inside my head snickers slyly and asks the question that I don't dare form out loud. *Aren't they?*

THIRTEEN

I wander off by myself, thinking about the Holocaust and what Burke said. I want to come back at him with a watertight argument, show him he was wrong to make such accusations about my dad. But I can't think of anything.

I don't pay much attention to the exhibits. Some of my mates tumble by, calling for me to join them, but I shake my head and keep to myself. I can't get that girl's book out of my mind. I keep imagining myself in her place, head bent over the pages, concentrating hard, unaware of the army of hateful Nazis bearing down upon me, surrounding the house, crashing in, taking me.

I push lower into the building, down the stairs to the World War I section, familiar from my previous visit. I wish I'd paid more attention before. If I had, maybe I'd understand about the two wars, how one led to the next, how other nations let the Nazis build and spread and do whatever they liked.

There's a trench recreation that I vaguely recall, a life-size model of what part of a real trench was like, to give an idea of the hellish conditions soldiers lived in before they went over the top to be ripped apart by machine guns. I stroll through the narrow, nightmarish maze, pausing to study the details, holes where soldiers slept, things they ate, fake rats.

In a strange way I feel better here. It helps distract me from the horrors upstairs. This war was brutal but human. Soldiers fought other soldiers. Millions died, but there were no death camps, no gas chambers. No little Jewish girls were rounded up, humiliated, tormented and executed.

If I could go back in time, I wouldn't mind stopping here, in the years before the truly horrific war began, before people found out just how demonically vile they could be. I could live with a war like this. But not the one that followed. And for Burke to say that my dad was no better than a Nazi ...

My blood boils and rushes to my cheeks. I won't let that insult drop. I'll tell Mrs Reed. Burke can't say things like that. If I rat on him, he'll be out of a job and good riddance to the bugger.

But as much as I'd like to hurt Burke, I don't want to do that. Partly because nobody likes a grass. But mostly because the stuff that he said got under my skin. I've always liked to think that I see things as they are. I know Dad's no saint, but I've never thought of him as a monster. But if Burke's right, and I take Dad's side, the way I've gone along with him for all these years, won't that make me a monster too?

I've told myself it doesn't matter that I never stood up to Dad. For the sake of a quiet life I've pretended to be on the same racist page as him. I didn't think it made a difference, letting a minor bigot spout off without challenging him. But I've been questioning that recently, even before what happened with Nancy.

Did people like me go along with the Nazis that way in the early days? Did other children put on an act for their fathers, figuring nothing bad could come of it? Can the terrors of that war in some way be traced back to the kids who didn't put their parents on the spot?

As I'm pondering my twisted relationship with Dad, I turn a corner and spot a struggle ahead. Two men are fighting with an Indian woman. She has a headscarf, a painted dot in the middle of her forehead, long flowing dress, the works. One of the men has a hand over her mouth. As I gawp at them, the other man hits her hard in the stomach and she goes down like a doll that's been dropped.

There's a baby in a pushchair, maybe a year old, a boy. He's crying. One of the men picks him up.

'Hey!' I shout. They glance around. It's dark in here and they're not that close to me. They're both wearing hoodies. I can't see their faces. 'What the hell are you doing?'

The men dart away from me, taking the baby. The woman moans and reaches out desperately, fingers opening and closing, clutching for the stolen boy.

I race after the men, not stopping to see if the woman's all right. There's no time to help her. If I lose sight of them, they'll disappear into the warren of the museum and that'll be the last I see of the child.

I hit the ground floor and hurry after the kidnappers. They've slowed slightly, so as not to draw attention to themselves. I want to roar, but I'm out of breath from fear and the race up the stairs.

I've almost caught up with them when one of the men stops and turns before the museum shop. He tackles me and tries to wrestle me to the floor. No time to fight fair. I scratch at his eyes. He hisses and his grip loosens. I make a bit of space for myself and knee him in the groin. He groans and collapses. I jump over him and push on, ignoring the astonished crowd around us, people staring, slack-jawed, a few of my friends among them.

Out front. No sign of the man with the baby. I look right, then left, and spot him streaking towards the giant cannons and the road beyond. I shout, 'Stop!' Then I run after him again.

The man halts before he gets to the cannons. Turns and waits. He's holding the baby close to his chest.

I come to a wary halt a few metres from him. He's not much bigger than me, but I don't want to take any chances. He might have a knife or a gun.

'Put down the baby,' I snarl.

In response the man pushes back his hood with his free hand. I feel my face go pale. He looks like a mutant out of a horror film. His skin is disfigured, purplish in patches, pustulent, some strips of flesh peeling from his cheeks. Straggly grey hair. Pale yellow eyes. He's missing some teeth, and those still intact are black and cracked.

He points at me and I note absent-mindedly that he doesn't have any fingernails, just filthy, bloodstained

flaps of skin. He stares, eyes widening, and crooks one of his fingers, like he's trying to hypnotise me.

I think about tackling the mutant, but I'm not gonna make the sort of dumb mistakes that people do in horror flicks. Taking a step back, I scream as loudly as I can, hoping that guards will come running.

Footsteps behind me. The man I knocked down outside the shop rushes past. He half-twirls and spits at me. He looks like a mutant too, like he's survived a nuclear war and is suffering from radiation poisoning. I think for a moment that the pair of freaks are going to attack me. But then I hear lots of people coming, muttering and shouting. A woman shrieks, 'My son! Don't hurt my son!'

The mutant holding the baby looks past me and his face twists with fury. He sets his sights on me again and leers. He licks his lips lewdly—his tongue is shrivelled and scabby.

As the footsteps draw closer, the man raises the baby high, then throws him at me. I grab the boy like a ball, cushioning him as best I can. I fall backwards and land on my bum. The baby sits in my lap and laughs, poking at my nose with his chubby little fingers.

I look up. The mutants have fled. They're moving fast now that they don't have the baby. They reach the gate and seconds later they're gone, out of sight.

Just before the crowd catches up with me, I stare into the baby's face. I half-expect him to smile sinisterly and say, '*don't be afraid mummy*,' like the babies in my dreams. But of course he doesn't. This is the real world, not a nightmare.

Then I think of the two men, their unnatural skin and yellow eyes. And I wonder.

FOURTEEN

I'm hailed as a hero by the baby's mother. She hugs me and thanks me through her sobs, saying I'm wonderful, I saved her child, I should get a reward. Strangers look on and beam. Guards and staff from the museum congratulate me. My mates from school watch, astonished. Burke is smiling. He winks when I catch his eye.

The guards try to get descriptions of the men from me. I tell them I didn't see much, that they didn't let their hoods drop. I don't tell them about the odd skin, the yellow eyes, that they looked like mutants. I'd sound like a lunatic if I did.

I shrug off the compliments on the Tube back to

school, scowling and saying nothing. Burke tells the others to leave me alone and I sit in silence, listening to the rumblings of the train, staring out of the window at the darkness of the tunnels, unable to forget the men's lips, their skin, those eyes. If I *did* imagine all that, I have a more vivid imagination than I ever gave myself credit for.

Back at school, Burke asks if I'm all right. When he sees that I'm not, he offers to take me home early. I don't want any special treatment, so I tell him I'd rather stay and I sit in an empty classroom for the rest of the afternoon. Burke and Mrs Reed pop in to see me a few times – Mrs Reed says I've done the school proud – but otherwise I'm alone with my thoughts. And if I could get away from them, I would.

The minutes drag but eventually pass and I slip out of school ahead of the bell, so as not to have to face my friends. I feel strange, like I've been violently sick. I just want to go home, rest up, stay in for the weekend, and hopefully return in better form on Monday.

Mum has already heard about the incident at the museum when I get back. She squeals when I walk in and calls me her little hero. Hugs and coos over me, asks if I want anything special for dinner. I grin weakly and tell her I don't have much of an appetite, I'll just have whatever she's having.

She wants me to tell her all about it, the kidnapping, the rescue, how I stood up to two grown men. I try to shrug it off, but she keeps on and on about it. Eventually I give in and start talking. I hold back the bit about how the men looked. I don't plan on telling anyone about that.

Dad gets home before I'm finished. He's grinning when he comes in and sees us chatting—he thinks we're gossiping. When Mum starts to tell him what happened, he frowns, tells her to shut up and makes me go through it again from the start.

Mum serves up dinner, fish and chips, usually my favourite, but they taste like cardboard in my current state. She keeps saying how brave I was, how she's proud of me, how the staff at the museum shouldn't have let me face a pair of dangerous criminals by myself.

Dad doesn't say much. He's got a face on him, the sort of scowl I know all too well. He's brooding about something. Mum's so excited, she doesn't clock it, but I do and I keep my trap shut, not wanting to wind him up any further. It's best to say as little as possible when he's in a mood like this.

It finally comes out when we're watching TV after dinner. Mum's still babbling about the baby and how I should get a medal. Dad sighs irritably and says, 'I wish you'd drop it, Daisy.'

'But aren't you proud, Todd?' Mum replies, surprised.

Dad grunts and shoots me a dirty look. I act as if I'm fascinated by the chef who's showing us how to cook a meal for six people in less than thirty minutes.

'Of course I'm pleased that you stood up for yourself,' he says to me. 'But . . .'

'What?' Mum huffs when he doesn't go on. I groan. Why doesn't she know when to keep quiet?

'They were Indian,' Dad says softly, and I look round. I didn't know what was gnawing at him before. Now it becomes clear.

'What's that got to do with anything?' Mum asks, bewildered.

'We'd be better off if they took a dozen little Indians and dumped them in the Thames.' Dad laughs, like he's only joking, but I know he's genuinely angry.

Mum frowns. 'Don't say things like that, Todd. It's not funny. It's not the poor baby's fault it's Indian.'

'It's not mine either, is it?' Dad snaps. He glares at Mum, then looks at me and grimaces. 'I like that you tried to help, but if it had been an English kid . . .'

'That's outrageous,' Mum says frostily. 'Babies are innocent. Would you have left the child to those two beasts?'

'Nobody's innocent,' Dad says. 'It's us against them.

Always has been, always will be. If we start fighting their battles for them, where will it stop? Do we let them stay because they have cute babies? Keep on giving them benefits, so they can spit out more of the buggers, until they have enough to outvote us? Babies grow up. They infest good schools and ruin them. They buy houses and destroy neighbourhoods. They import drugs and sell them to our kids. They blow things up.

'They were all babies once,' Dad says. 'Every last terrorist and job-stealing scab was like that boy in the museum. We can't be soft. We can't give ground. *Ever.*'

'You're wrong,' Mum says and I think Dad's even more amazed than I am. She's never spoken to him like this before. I wouldn't have thought that she could. 'There are bad people in the world, Todd, white as well as coloured. We can't let people steal babies. We'd be cruel if we –'

Dad's hand shoots up and he slaps her hard. Her head cracks back and she cries out. He grabs her throat and squeezes. His eyes are wild. I throw myself at him, roaring at him to stop. He hits me with his free hand, slaps me even harder than he slapped Mum. I'm knocked to the floor by the force of the blow, but Dad barely notices. He's fully fixed on Mum.

'Don't ever talk to me that way,' Dad snarls. 'I won't

have you turn on me. If you ever stick up for those bastards again, I'll kill you. You hear me, woman? Do. You. Bloody. Well. *Hear. Me?*'

He shakes her with every word. Mum makes a choking noise and tries to nod. Her fingers scratch at his arms. For a moment I think he's gonna finish her off, that this is how it will end. All these years, all the beatings, all leading to this. I push myself to my feet, ready to lunge at him again, desperate to stop him, to save Mum, to escape with her before he can make good on his threat.

But then Dad's fingers relax and withdraw. He clutches Mum's chin and gives her the evil eyeball. She's weeping. Her nose is bleeding. The flesh under her left eye is already starting to puff up. Dad wipes blood from her lip and smiles tightly.

'You'll be all right,' he says as if she'd just tripped and hurt herself. 'Go make us all a cuppa. Have a fag out back. You'll be fine when you come in. Won't you?'

Mum gasps repeatedly like a dying fish. Dad's fingers clench.

'*Won't you?*' he barks, sharper this time, wanting to hear an answer.

'Yes . . . Todd,' Mum wheezes.

Dad releases her. She gets up and stumbles to the

kitchen, trying not to sob, knowing that if she makes too much noise, it will infuriate him and maybe set him off again.

Dad looks at me and I wait for him to follow up his first blow. If he lays into me, I'll just stand here and let him beat me. It's the best thing to do. He loses his rag completely if I fight back. I don't mind the beatings, the pain. As long as Mum's out of the way and safe, he can hit me as hard as he likes.

'I'll say this though,' Dad says slowly, then pauses, letting me know that he could swing either way right now, that he can laugh this off or come down hard on me, that he has the power, that me and Mum are his to control. 'I wish I'd been there to see you knee that sod.'

We both laugh, Dad loudly, me weakly. He switches channels to a quiz show, gets a few answers right and chuckles proudly, delighted with himself. Mum brings the tea and he pats her bum as she places it before him. She smiles crookedly, sits by his side and kisses the hand he struck her with.

Later, in my room, sitting up in bed, listening to tunes on my iPod. Crying. I hate tears, but tonight I can't hold them back. I'm not in much pain – the slap didn't even leave a mark – but inside I feel wretched.

I don't want to blame Dad for what he did. I make excuses for him, the way I always do. Mum shouldn't have challenged him. She knows what he's like. She should have read his mood and ...

No. I can't lay the blame on her. I was wrong too. I shouldn't have risked my neck for an Indian kid. I should have left the baby to the mutants. One less for us to kick out of the country. Dad was right. He was trying to help us see the world the way it really is. We should have listened. It wasn't his fault. I shouldn't have saved the baby. Mum should have kept her mouth shut.

I tell myself that over and over. I make every excuse for him that I can. And I try to believe. I try so bloody hard to justify his actions, because he's my dad and I love him. But deep down I know it's a load of bull.

When I'm crying so hard that I'm making moaning sounds, I channel the music through my speakers so that Dad won't hear. Then I weep harder, fingers balled into fists, face scrunched up with hate and confusion.

He's a bully. A wife-beater. A racist. A hateful, nasty sod. I want to hang him up by his thumbs. Sneer at him as he writhes in agony. Ask him if he's proud of himself now, if he still thinks it's all right to beat up a woman and child.

Then I despise myself for thinking such a terrible thing. He wants what's best for us. He's trying to help, doing all that he can to steer us the right way. He only hits us when we let him down. We have to try harder. We . . .

'I hate him,' I moan, burying my face in my hands.

But he's my dad.

'I hate him.'

But he's my dad.

'I hate him.'

But . . .

FIFTEEN

Saturday drags. I stay in all day. A few of my mates call and ask me to come meet up, but I tell them I don't feel well. They say everyone's talking about me and how I rescued the baby. I laugh it off like it's no big deal.

Dad takes us out to a Chinese restaurant for dinner. Mum dresses up and slaps make-up over her bruise. She and Dad share a couple of bottles of wine. He lets me have a sip when nobody's watching. Laughs when I grimace.

'Don't worry,' he says. 'You'll get used to it.'

Dad's polite as he can be to the staff. Funny how he doesn't have a problem with foreigners when they're serving him food. Most of his favourite grub comes from overseas, Chinese, Italian, Indian. I consider pointing that out, but I don't want to set him off again.

Mum and Dad head to the pub after the meal, leaving me to hold the fort at home. Dad gives me a fiver and tells me to treat myself to some crisps and sweets. He scratches my head and grins. I grin back. The aggro of yesterday isn't forgotten by any of us, but we move on, the way we always do. No point living in the past. We'd have burnt out long ago if we held grudges.

I watch a film, surf the web, download some new tracks, play a few games, go to bed late. I don't hear the old pair come home.

I get up about midday. Dad's still asleep. Mum's working on a Sunday roast. We're a bit stiff with each other. It always takes us a while to return to normal after Dad loses his temper. We're both embarrassed.

We eat at two. Dad's hung-over, but he still manages to polish off his plate. He loves roasts, never leaves more than scraps. He drinks beer with the dinner, saying that's the only way to combat a hangover. Normally he praises Mum's cooking, but he doesn't say much today, nursing a headache.

'That was nice,' I mutter as Mum clears up.

'I've got dessert for later,' Mum smiles. 'Pavlova. Your favourite.'

It's actually Dad's favourite, but I don't mind. We share a smile. Things are getting better. The air doesn't feel so tight around me now.

Dad watches football in the afternoon. I watch some of the match with him. I make a few scathing comments about Premiership players and how they're overpaid prima donnas. That's usually guaranteed to set him off on an enthusiastic rant, but today he just grunts, wincing every now and then, rubbing his head as if that will make the pain go away.

Some of Mum's friends come to visit. They don't say anything about her face, don't even ask if she had an accident. They start chirping about what happened at the War Museum, but Mum shushes them before Dad kicks off again. They retreat to the kitchen and carry on in whispers.

I go to my room when the football's over and phone Vinyl, hoping he won't have heard about the museum. No such luck.

'I hear you're London's newest superhero,' he chuckles.

'Get stuffed.'

'They should send you over to Ireland to stamp out the zombies.'

'Don't make me come and give you a kicking,' I warn him.

He asks if I've heard the latest rumours. Apparently Pallaskenry wasn't the first place the zombies struck. According to supposedly classified documents which have somehow surfaced on the internet, there were at least three other attacks in small, out-of-the-way villages, one in Africa, two in South America.

'If that's true,' Vinyl says, 'you can bet there's been even more of them in places we haven't heard of yet.'

'It's all crap,' I tell him. 'They're trying to scare us.'

'Maybe,' he hums. 'But it looks like the curfew's going ahead. They've already introduced it in a lot of towns in Wales, since that's so close to Ireland. London nightlife's gonna be a thing of the past soon.'

'That won't last,' I snort. 'You think people here will stand for a lockdown? I give it a week or less. The rumours will die away, the curfew will be lifted, everything will go back to normal.'

'I hope so,' he sighs.

We chat about TV and music. I tell Vinyl how Nancy confronted me at school, treating me like a racist. I get huffy about it, conveniently not mentioning the fact that I made gorilla noises. Vinyl isn't in the least sympathetic.

'Well, you *are* a racist,' he notes.

'No, I'm not,' I snap. 'I'm talking to you, and you're hardly Snow White.'

'I'm your token black friend,' he chuckles.

'No,' I sniff. 'You're my token retarded friend.'

I hang up before he can yell at me. Giggling wickedly, delighted to have trumped him, I punch the air, then go take a long, hot bath. There's nothing like a good soak when it comes to relaxing. I lie in the tub for an hour, staring at the drops of condensation on the ceiling and window, feeling peaceful. The old scar on my thigh is itchy, so I scratch it, then turn on my side and let the air at it. When it stops annoying me, I lie flat again.

Mum and I watch TV together later. Dad's gone out to the pub. Mum opens a box of chocolates and we share them. Belgian chocs. They're nice, but I prefer Roses or Quality Street. You can't beat a good Strawberry Cream.

Dad gets back with a few of his mates not long after ten. My stomach tenses when they enter – I think Owl Man is going to be with them – but these are just some of his campaign buddies. They have posters and leaflets. Local elections aren't for another three or four months, but they've been asked to start canvassing early. One of the posters has a picture of a zombie, set next to a photo of a Muslim bomber. *Which do you fear most?* it asks.

Dad and his mates love the poster. Mum and I pretend to admire it too. Then we go to bed early. Dad doesn't like us hanging around when he's talking shop. I'm sure that I'll struggle to drop off, or have the nightmare again, but I don't. I'm out in a minute and sleep the sleep of the dead after that.

SIXTEEN

I could do without school on Monday. I think about giving it a miss – wouldn't be the first time – but I don't fancy the idea of trudging round the streets by myself. If I'd met up with my mates over the weekend, I could have arranged for a few of them to skip school with me. But it's too late to organise that now, so I decide to struggle through and maybe take tomorrow off instead.

Everyone's still talking about the museum, the way I rescued the baby. Suze and La Lips shiver when they ask me to recreate it for them, eyes wide, wanting a tale of blood, treachery and heroism.

'It wasn't much,' I mutter. 'The guys weren't that big.'

'Rubbish,' Kray says. 'I saw the one you tackled outside the shop. He was well over six foot. That knee put him down sweet though.'

Kray's not the only one living in awe of my trusty right knee. I reckon some of the fools would kneel down and kiss it if I gave them the chance.

The praise goes to my head a bit, but my mood doesn't lift. No matter how many times I'm told that I'm a hero, I can't forget about Dad, the contempt in his expression, the way he hit Mum and me. If ever there was a time to stand up to him and tell him I'm not a racist, it was then. I could have said that I thought all babies were equal. Attacked him for being so heartless, so inhuman.

Instead I just stood there, head low, saying nothing. As always.

It's almost a relief to get to class. I can escape from the adulation there. We have biology first. I'm worried that Mr Burke might make a song and dance about what I did at the museum, but he's not in today, must be sick. Mrs Reed takes our class instead.

The morning rolls along drearily. I trudge from one class to the next, ignoring anyone who tries to talk to me about Friday, scribbling during lessons, paying little or no attention to the teachers.

I meet up with some of the gang during break and I'm delighted when Elephant draws their attention away from me.

'I'm playing football at lunch,' he beams. 'Saw the doctor on Friday and she gave me the all-clear. Said it'll probably hurt for a few days, and not to tackle too hard, but I've got the green light.'

Elephant's so excited, you'd swear he was about to play in a Cup Final, not in a poxy five-a-side tournament. We slag him a bit, but he laughs off our jeers, vowing to score a hat-trick and come back bigger and better than ever.

'*Bigger?*' La Lips says, batting her eyelids innocently.

We all laugh, even the normally jealous Copper.

Elephant makes us promise to come and cheer him on. I normally wouldn't bother with footie at lunch, but to keep Elephant happy, I agree to watch him make a fool of himself.

'Just don't elbow anybody,' Suze warns him, 'or B will go for you.'

Elephant looks blank. He must be the only person not to have heard about the incident on Friday. Luckily, before I'm forced to go through it again for his benefit, the bell rings and it's back to class.

More pointless lessons, teachers droning on, trying to

amuse myself by drawing crude cartoons and coming up with nicknames for the few of my friends who don't have any. Then lunch.

I head to the gym with Copper, Kray, Suze, La Lips, Ballydefeck and Stagger Lee. We meet Pox, Trev and Linzer there. Elephant's warming up. Meths is on his team and the two of them hold a hushed conversation, discussing tactics. What a pair of wallies!

Stuttering Stan is the ref. He blows his whistle and the teams take to the pitch. Other kids move out of their way and either line up along the sides to watch or go find somewhere else to hang out.

The game kicks off and Elephant gets stuck straight in. If anyone expected him to take things easy in his first game back, they're instantly corrected as he goes into a tackle feet first and barges one of the other players over.

Stuttering Stan blows for a free kick and gives Elephant a warning. Elephant rubs his leg and looks worried. As soon as Stuttering Stan's back is turned, he winks at Meths. I see now what they were cooking up— play the wounded soldier angle, use Stuttering Stan's sympathy to get away with as many dirty tackles as they can.

'Go on, Elephant!' I roar as he chases the action. 'Do him!'

The others cheer along with me. The goalie pulls off a save and launches the ball up the pitch to Elephant. He turns, shoots and almost scores the goal of his life, but it flies just a few centimetres over.

We're having a great time. For once I'm immersed, keen to see who Elephant targets next, if he can cap his comeback with a goal, how much grimacing and sighing Stuttering Stan will stand for before he brandishes a yellow card.

Then Tyler Bayor spoils it all. He sidles up to me and gives my sleeve a tug. I glance at him suspiciously. He's never approached me like this before. I figure I must be in trouble, that he's delivering a message for someone.

'What do you want?' I snap.

Tyler grins shakily. 'I just wanted to say well done for the other day.'

I stare at him incredulously. The others are amazed too. He must have fallen out of bed and hit his head this morning. It's madness, tagging me like this, acting like we can be friends, that a compliment from him can make everything right between us. Who the hell does he reckon he is, Nelson bloody Mandela?

'Do you think I give a damn what you think of me?' I snarl.

Tyler's face creases and he gulps. 'No, B, of course not. I just wanted to –'

I poke him in the chest and he takes a quick step back. I follow and the gang closes around me, their focus switching from the game to the new, more highly-charged action.

'Who gave you permission to breathe the same air as me?' I sneer, poking Tyler again.

'Why are you doing this?' he whines. 'I only wanted to tell you that I thought it was great, the way you saved that kid.'

'I didn't do it to please the likes of you,' I tell him. 'In fact, if I'd known the baby was Indian, I'd have let them take him.'

Snickers and theatrical gasps from the gang. They think I'm joking, saying it to wind Tyler up. They don't know about what happened at home, how serious this is. If I let Tyler praise me, it'll be like I'm taking his side against Dad.

'All right,' Tyler sighs. 'I'm sorry. I won't congratulate you again.'

He turns to leave. I grab his arm and swing him back to face me.

'You're not going anywhere.' I poke his chest a third time. 'You started this. Let's take it all the way.'

Tyler's eyes fill with panic. I've given him a rough ride over the years, but I've never gone all out for him. He's small. I don't usually pick fights with no-hopers. I go for opponents who stand a chance, who are worth beating. Tyler isn't a fighter. He probably thought he'd never get called out by me.

But he rubbed me up the wrong way at the wrong time. I know it's unfair. It's my dad I should be squaring up to, not a wimp like Tyler. Or if not Dad, then one of Tyler's bigger buddies, someone who could give as good as he gets. But I can't help myself. I've been bottling in my anger all weekend. I have to lash out at someone and Tyler's placed himself in my line of fire.

'Easy, B,' Trev mutters, seeing something dark flash across my face.

'You want some of this too?' I bark.

He shakes his head and goes quiet.

I focus on Tyler again. I'm snarling like a dog. Tyler looks like he's about to faint. Before he passes out, I slap him, the way his mate Nancy slapped me when I made the gorilla noises.

'Come on,' I hiss. 'Show me what you've got.'

'I don't want to fight,' Tyler says, backing up.

'Too bad.' I slap him again. 'Give me your best shot.'

'No,' he squeals. 'I don't want to.'

I make a fist and jab him in the stomach. It's not a hard punch, just a taste of things to come. But he doubles over, then drops to his knees and starts crying, hugging himself as if I'd swung a cricket bat into his ribs.

I stare at Tyler uncertainly. I'm not used to this sort of reaction. It throws me. The others are looking away, clearing their throats, disgusted and embarrassed at the same time. This is doing more harm to my image than Tyler's. Everyone knows he's soft. But for me to pick a fight with a harmless crybaby . . .

'Forget about him,' I snap, turning my back on Tyler and looking for another target. I spot a group of Muslim kids standing in a huddle, unaware of any of this, sharing a joke. They're from the year above ours, big buggers, well able to fight their corner.

'Let's do those bastards,' I snarl, looking to my gang for support.

Nobody responds. They're startled by my sudden mood swing, my thirst for a fight. They've seen me fired up before, but not like this.

'What's wrong?' I sneer. 'Frightened?'

'Of course not,' Kray says. 'But why don't we leave it and have a go at them after school instead? We'll get in trouble if we attack them here.'

He's right, but I can't pull back now. 'OK, cowards,' I spit. 'I'll do the sods myself.'

I start towards the group. I don't know if the others will follow once they see that I'm serious. I'll get hammered to a pulp if they don't—without backup I won't stand a chance. But I don't care. Let them kick the crap out of me. At least I'll be able to go home to Dad and be sure of a warm welcome. He'll make me a cup of tea, rub my head, tell me I'm one of his own. He might criticise me for picking a fight I couldn't win, and tell me I have to be cannier. But he'll be proud of me. He'll love my fighting spirit. He'll love *me*. And right now that's all in the world that matters.

But I haven't taken more than three steps when everything goes to hell and all natural fights are forgotten.

Screams ring out loud over the other noises. Everyone stops and stares at the main doors into the gym. They're hanging open and we can see the corridor beyond. The screams get louder. My eyes widen and my heart beats fast. I instinctively know what this means, but I can't admit it. Nobody can. That's why we stand like a bunch of dummies, doing nothing.

A boy staggers into the gym. He's bleeding. Terrified. Moaning. He falls and I see that a chunk has been cut – *bitten* – out of the back of his neck. Blood spurts from the wound. As we gawp, more kids spill into the gym. All screaming. Some bleeding. Everyone in shock.

One of the girls looks wild-eyed at the rest of us, as if just noticing we're there. Gazes at us in horrified silence. Then shrieks hysterically—'*Zombies!*'

SEVENTEEN

I want it to be a joke, some smart-arses screwing with the rest of us. I'd be so happy if they were winding us up, I wouldn't care that I'd been made a fool of. I'd laugh, admit I fell for it, hail them as champion pranksters.

But the blood's real. The terror. The screams.

And the zombies.

I spot the first of them coming. A boy I don't recognise. His jumper and shirt are ripped. His stomach has been carved open. Guts ooze from holes as he lurches forward. His eyes are unfocused, his lips caked with blood. He moves stiffly but purposefully.

The undead boy grabs the girl who screamed. Pulls

her hair back. Sinks his teeth into her throat. Rips out a strip of flesh and gurgles happily as blood sprays his face.

I've seen blood fly in fights, movies and computer games. But never like this. Nothing I've ever seen before has prepared me for *this*.

The spell breaks and pandemonium erupts. Everyone's screaming at once. People run in circles, crash into one another, fall, thrash around on the ground, lash out with their feet and fists.

More zombies stream into the gym, boys, girls, a couple of teachers. They zone in on the living, hunting like wolves. They have a sweet time of it. In all the mayhem, lots of kids try to rush by them. Easy prey. The zombies just reach out and snatch.

I haven't moved. I'm watching sickly, numbly studying the undead as they feast on their victims. Some of the kids writhe and swear as they're bitten, moan and weep and beg for mercy. The zombies don't care. They tear with their fingers and teeth, bite, claw, rip, chew.

'Stop that!' Stuttering Stan roars. He strides forward, blowing his whistle, trying to wave back the zombies. The fool thinks that he can control this, the same way he can control violence on the pitch.

A zombie boy my age butts Stuttering Stan in the

chest. As the teacher falls back, winded, the boy sticks his fingers into the adult's left eye and pokes it out. As Stuttering Stan screams, the boy gobbles the eye. Then he falls on his victim and digs through the hole where the eye should be, burrowing through to Stuttering Stan's brain.

'Come on!' Trev shouts, grabbing my arm. 'We have to get out of here!'

'What?' I blink.

'They're gonna kill us, B!'

I look at the zombies and shake my head. 'Not all of us. There's a pattern.'

'What the hell are you talking about?' he barks.

I point. The zombies aren't killing everyone. As each one enters the gym, he or she cuts or bites a few people, leaving them to yell and flee. Only then does the zombie settle on a target, break their skull and dig into their brain. Once they start to feast, they sit there, gorging, ignorant of everything going on around them.

'There's a pattern,' I mutter again.

Before I can make sense of it, Trev shouts, 'We're going. You can stay and let them eat you if you want.'

I glance at him and the others in our gang. They're racing towards the rear left corner of the gym. My senses click—there's an emergency exit there.

I stare at the carnage, the kids going wild, the zombies tucking in. I was in a daze before this, detached and calm. But now that I focus, I realise I'm dead if I don't move quickly.

'Sod this!' I moan, then tear after the others as fast as I can.

EIGHTEEN

The gym is situated at the back of the school. There are several buildings behind it, shops and a factory. No direct way through, except for a narrow alley included at the insistence of the local authorities.

Trev's ducking through a small door when I catch up. The others have gone ahead. He looks back as I rush after him, afraid I'm a zombie. He smiles fleetingly when he recognises me, then stands aside and lets me pass.

'This way!' he yells, waving his arms over his head.

'What are you doing?' I snap.

'We've got to help the rest of them,' he pants.

I study the scores of students fighting with those

who've been turned into zombies. Lots are trying to escape through the main doors. Some are trying to climb the walls, to get to the skylight windows which lead to the roof, but they've no hope—too smooth, too high, no ladders or ropes. Others have collapsed mentally and huddle on the floor, weeping, praying, shaking their heads, hoping the zombies will leave them alone or that they'll wake up and find out this was just a dream.

'Forget about them,' I tell Trev.

'But we can't just –'

'If you keep on shouting, you'll alert the zombies. You want them coming after us?' He stares at me, tears in his eyes. 'Best thing we can do is get out and call for help, Trev. It's their only hope.'

Trev looks round the gym, then swears and shoves through after me.

We're in a small corridor, me, Trev, Ballydefeck, Suze, La Lips, Elephant, Meths, Linzer, Copper, Stagger Lee, Pox, Dunglop. Tyler's with us too, and a few others, two black guys, an Indian, three Muslims, a white kid called Rick.

'Where's Kray?' Trev asks.

'One of them got him,' Suze sobs. 'It cracked his head open. I saw it ... his brains ... it ...'

'What the hell's going on?' the tallest of the black kids roars. 'How'd they get in? Where'd they come from? I thought they only came out at night.'

We stare at him in silence. Then I shrug. 'We'll ask questions later. Let's get out of here before the brain-munching bastards find us.'

We hurry down the corridor. The emergency exit's at the end. It opens out into the alley which runs between the two buildings behind the school. I've been through it a few times during fire drills. Never thought I'd have to do this for real, or that I'd be running from zombies, not a fire.

Ballydefeck gets to the door first. He slams down on the access bar and pushes.

Nothing happens.

'Out of the way,' the tall black guy snaps. He bangs the bar down and shoves hard.

Nothing happens.

'Everyone,' I shout. 'Push together.'

We crowd round the door. I get some fingers on the bar. It slides down smoothly when we push, but the door doesn't give, not even a crack.

'Forget the bar,' Trev says. 'Focus on the door.'

We strain, silent, red-faced, sweating, shoving with everything we have.

The door doesn't move.

'It's jammed shut,' Ballydefeck says.

'Can we cut through?' Tyler asks.

'With what?' Pox yells. He got his nickname because of the spattering of facial scars left behind when he had chickenpox. The scars aren't normally very prominent, but now that his face is scrunched up with terror, he looks like a rabid monkey. I almost make a joke about it, but this isn't the time to be a wisearse.

'We're all gonna die,' La Lips wails.

'Shut up,' I tell her. 'Trev?' I look to him, hoping he'll have an answer.

'There's another exit to the alley on this side of the building, on the floor above,' he says. 'Or there's the front door.'

'Which do you think we should –'

A scream stops me. My head whips round. A small girl is dangling from Pox's right arm, teeth locked on his flesh, chewing her way down to the bone.

Pox screams again and slams the girl into the wall. She doesn't let go. He jabs at her face with the fingers of his free hand. In a swift movement she releases him and snaps at his fingers. Catches them and grinds down. Pox screams louder and falls to his knees.

I start towards them, but the black kid who beat me

to the bar beats me to the girl too. There's a flick knife in his right hand. He slashes the blade across the girl's chest. She loses interest in Pox and pushes her attacker away. Looks at the gash in her chest. Gurgles, then throws herself at the teenager with the knife.

He keeps his cool. Ducks the girl's attack, then jabs the knife at her face. She winces when it strikes. He winces too. I can see horror in his eyes. He's never done anything like this before. But when the zombie snaps at his fingers, he thrusts the horror away, grits his teeth and digs the knife deeper into her head. She swipes at him, squealing and snapping at his fingers.

'Hold her down!' he roars.

Trev and I react quickest and wrestle her to the floor. She snaps at the black kid again, but he keeps his fingers clear of her mouth. Drives the knife deep into her head, panting like a dog. Again. Blood flows. Bone splinters. He doesn't stop. Moments later he's gouging out chunks of brain, making sobbing noises. The girl shudders, moans, spasms. He keeps it up, face grim, silent now, teeth bared. Finally she stops moving and her eyes go steady in their sockets.

'Is she dead?' Trev asks.

'Yeah,' the guy croaks, getting up, wiping tears from his cheeks. He's trembling wildly, his left hand shaking like mad. But his right hand – his knife hand – is steady as the blade itself.

'How can we be sure?' Stagger Lee asks.

'I destroyed her brain,' the black kid grunts.

'That works in movies, but we don't know for sure that it happens that way in real life,' I note, eyeing the dead girl nervously. 'What if she comes back to life and attacks again?'

He laughs edgily. 'Then we're screwed.'

I look up, shocked, then laugh with him. It's that or go mad.

'How'd you sneak in the knife?' I ask.

'I never leave home without it. Been mugged too many times.'

'If the teachers found it . . .'

'That lot don't know how to find their own arse-holes.'

My smile spreads. 'I'm B,' I tell him.

'Cass.'

'Isn't that a girl's name?'

'Short for Cassius. After Muhammad Ali's real name.'

'Sweet.' I show my knuckles and let him knock them.

'We killed her,' Suze cries.

'We had to,' Cass says, then takes a deep, steadying breath. 'We've gotta get out of here.'

'But –' Suze says.

'Shut it,' Meths snarls. He's still holding the football which he must have picked up when the game stopped.

'Are you all right?' I ask Pox.

He's bleeding, shaking like an old geezer with Parkinson's, even worse than Cass was, but he nods. 'I'll live,' he moans, taking off his jumper and using it to wipe blood from his arm and fingers.

'But as what?' Cass says, blade still extended, pointing now at Pox.

'What do you mean?' Pox frowns.

'We've all seen zombie films. You've been bitten. If you turn into one of them . . .'

'I won't!' Pox squeaks. As Cass glares at him, Pox looks for support. 'B? You're not gonna let him do me, are you?'

I glance at the others, but nobody meets my eye, happy to leave the decision to me now that it's been placed in my hands. Bloody cowards.

'B?' Pox wheezes, real terror in his eyes, fresh tears trickling down his cheeks and gathering in the pockmarks in his flesh. 'Are you gonna . . .?'

'No,' I mutter. 'But keep behind the rest of us, all right? And if we think you're starting to change, we'll have to cut you loose.'

'But –'

'No time to argue, Pox. Accept the rules or it's the knife.' I turn to Cass. 'What do you reckon—make a break for one of the exits or find a place to hole up and wait for help to arrive?'

'Nobody helped those buggers in Pallaskenry,' Copper says. 'The only ones who made it out alive were those who got out early. The soldiers surrounded the place once they hit the scene and shot anyone who moved, normal people along with the zombies.'

'Run?' Cass asks.

'Run,' I agree.

And we're off.

NINETEEN

We don't get very far. This corridor stretches along the side of the gym. We hurry to the end of it and start down the next passageway, off which lie a series of classrooms. But we're less than a quarter of the way along when we hear a mob racing towards us, screaming and wailing.

'They must be heading for the exit or the gym,' Stagger Lee says.

'They'll be on us in a sec,' Copper mutters.

'We have to tell them to go back,' Suze pants.

'Don't be stupid,' I snarl. 'They're being chased. They won't stop and listen calmly.'

'We won't get through them,' Cass says.

'Even if we do, zombies must be right behind,' Copper says.

There's a door to my left. I open it and glance into a small classroom for younger kids. It's empty.

'In here,' I decide. 'We'll hide, wait for them to pass, then sneak out.'

'What if the zombies smell us?' Cass asks.

I shrug. 'It's a gamble one way or the other.'

The first few kids of the mob surge into the hallway. Zombies are among them, snapping, tearing, maiming, killing. 'In!' I bark and everyone pushes into the room after me, no complaints.

When we're all inside, I slam the door shut. There's no key of course. 'We need to barricade it,' I shout, but some of the others are ahead of me. Copper and Ballydefeck arrive seconds later with a desk each, which they prop against the door. More furniture is added to the pile and moments later there's a mountain of desks and chairs between us and the door.

'Won't do much good if they come through the windows,' Trev says, nodding at the frosted glass on either side of the door.

'They can't see us through the glass,' I mutter, stepping back. 'And if we keep quiet, they can't hear us either.'

'What about smell?' Cass asks.

I frown. 'What is it with you and zombies smelling us?'

'I've seen movies where they can sniff out the living,' he says.

'Well, let's hope they all had really bad colds when they were turned,' I growl and we squat quietly.

Screams in the corridor. Sounds of fighting. Someone slams into the glass and it rattles. At first I think it's a zombie trying to break through, but it must have just been someone crashing into it, because there aren't any more assaults on the window.

'Please don't eat me!' I hear a kid beg. 'Please don't eat me! Please don't–'

A high-pitched shriek. I shut my eyes and feel tears build behind my eyelids. This can't be happening. Zombies aren't real. Pallaskenry was a joke. We were so sneery, laughing about it in class, coming up with alternative theories. I must be dreaming. Babies will come crawling over the desks any minute now, calling me their mummy, and I'll know it's a nightmare.

But that's wishful thinking. This is reality. I always know when I'm having a dream. No matter how real it seems at the time, it never *feels* completely real. This does.

I open my eyes and look around. Everyone's shaking and either crying or close to it. La Lips is clinging to Copper, weeping as he whispers soothing words in her ear. Linzer's praying. She's not the only one—Dunglop, Tyler, Ballydefeck and two of the Muslims are also openly praying. I figure some of the others are too, but privately.

Pox is squatting a couple of metres away from the rest of us, weeping over his wounds, shaking his head, muttering something beneath his breath. Cass is keeping an eye on him, flick knife open and glinting, ready to leap on Pox at the first sign that he's turning into a zombie.

'You know the worst thing about this?' Elephant whispers. When a few of us stare at him, he says glumly, 'It ruined my comeback.'

I stifle a giggle. 'Idiot!' I snort.

'You were crap anyway,' Meths says.

'Less of it,' Elephant growls.

'We need a plan,' Trev says and we look at him expectantly. 'We can't just go charging about the place.'

'So what should we do?' Cass asks.

'Stay here,' Trev says. 'Keep our heads down. Wait for the police to find us.'

'But in Pallaskenry –' Copper starts to object.

'This isn't Pallaskenry,' Trev snaps. 'It's a school.

They're not going to stand by and let soldiers kill a load of kids. There'd be riots if they did. They'll come as soon as they can, flush out the place, protect the survivors. If we can stay hidden for an hour or two, that's all we'll need. Maybe less.'

We consider Trev's plan.

'If police and soldiers raid the school,' Linzer says, 'we'd be safer here than out there. They shot anyone who moved in Ireland. They won't know who's a zombie and who isn't, and they won't want to take chances.'

'It'll be a free-for-all,' Copper agrees.

'But if the zombies find us first ...' Stagger Lee mutters. 'I say we make a break for it. Head for the stairs, get to the floor above, find the exit, let ourselves out, don't look back.'

'What if that door's shut too?' one of the Muslim boys asks.

'It won't be,' Stagger Lee says.

'The one by the gym was,' the Muslim reminds him.

'That was bad luck,' Stagger Lee says. 'There's no chance that two of the exits will be jammed at the same time.'

'Who says it was luck?' the Muslim asks. 'Am I the only one who thinks this is too much of a coincidence?

The caretakers check those doors regularly—they have to be sure they're working, in case of a fire. And on the very day we need them, one just happens to be stuck? I don't buy it.'

'What are you talking about?' Trev snaps.

'Someone sealed it shut,' the Muslim says. 'We've been locked in.'

A scary silence settles over us. I find myself looking at Cass and he looks back at me. His eyes are wider with fear than they were a minute ago.

'What's your name?' I ask the Muslim.

'Seez,' he says.

'Seez, do us all a favour and shut up,' I tell him.

'Why?' he scowls.

'If you're right, we're screwed,' I say evenly. 'So let's not think about it, and keep our fingers crossed that you're wrong.'

'But –'

'If we're locked in here with a pack of rotten zombies, what good will worrying about it do us?' I challenge him.

'We can come up with a plan,' he says.

I laugh bitterly. 'If someone's blocked all the exits, there's no plan, we're done for. We have to believe that the door back there was a one-off. If it wasn't, we'll find out soon enough and we won't have to worry about it for long.'

Seez stares at me, then nods reluctantly.

'So what do we do?' I ask. 'Hole up or try for the exits? Let's vote. Who wants to stay?'

Everyone looks around, hesitant to be the first to vote. Then Linzer sticks up her hand. A few more start to rise. But before a decision can be made, Pox groans, turns aside and vomits.

'Gross,' Dunglop chuckles—he's closest to Pox.

There's a strange creaking sound, like a plank being bent to snapping point. As I'm trying to place it, Pox shudders then falls still. The noise comes again. Cass takes a cautious step towards the motionless Pox, rolling his knife lightly between his fingers.

'Everyone stay back,' Cass says. 'I'm gonna make sure –'

Pox lurches to his feet, leaps at Dunglop and bites a chunk of flesh out of his cheek.

Dunglop screams and staggers into Cass, knocking him aside. Pox is already moving. He scrabbles after Rick, the kid from a lower year, and grabs his foot. Rick kicks out, but Pox bites into his ankle. As Rick screams, Pox turns on Suze and goes for her throat.

Cass gets in the way and jabs at Pox with his knife.

Pox lowers his head and charges. I tackle him before he connects with Cass. Drive him sideways. He crashes into a desk and goes sprawling.

'Clear the bloody door!' I roar. As the others hurry to the piled-up desks and chairs, I face Pox, who's back on his feet, snarling. There's a strange green fungus growing over the places where he was bitten by the zombie. Only thin wisps, but I note their presence like some super-sleuth with a keen eye for detail. And his fingernails are longer than they were.

No . . . hold on . . . those aren't nails. Bits of bone are sticking out of each finger, scraps of flesh and nails shedding from them. I recall the creaking noise and put two and two together. The bones must have lengthened and snapped through his flesh as he was changing. I glance down and spot bones sticking through the tips of his shoes too.

Pox closes in on me, but is distracted when Cass whistles.

'Here, boy,' Cass growls, beckoning Pox on. 'Come and get it.'

Pox scowls and goes after Cass, moving speedily. Cass stabs at him. The blade sinks deep into Pox's chest. It pierces his heart, but that doesn't matter to Pox. He pushes on and Cass goes down. Pox opens his jaws and snaps at Cass's face. His teeth are longer and thicker than I remember.

One of the Muslims grabs Pox before he can bite. Pulls him off Cass and pushes him away. Pox falls, but one of his bony nails scratches the Muslim's chin and draws blood.

'We're out of here!' Trev shouts and I see that the door is open. Everyone's spilling into the corridor. Meths is dragging Rick, and Dunglop is stumbling after the others.

'Let me help you,' I pant, taking Dunglop's arm.

'Thanks,' he moans, holding a hand to his bitten cheek.

'I'm so sorry,' I whisper, then whirl swiftly and send Dunglop flying across the room. He smashes into Pox, who goes down again and starts biting instinctively.

'What the hell!' Trev shouts.

'Meths!' I bark. 'Leave him.'

Meths looks at me uncertainly.

'They were bitten,' I growl. 'The same thing that happened to Pox will happen to them.'

'No!' Rick screams. 'Don't leave me! I won't change! You can't just –'

'B's right,' Copper says.

'Look,' La Lips groans, pointing.

Pox is tucking into Dunglop's brain. He's broken through the skull with the bones sticking out of his fingers and is gorging himself on the juicy stuff inside, like a pig chowing down. Dunglop's still alive, shivering, eyelids flickering with terror and shock. But he doesn't scream. Just spasms.

Meths drops Rick and backs away from him. When Rick tries to crawl after him, Meths kicks him in the head and the boy collapses with a whine.

Seez is staring at the scratched Muslim, who wipes drops of blood from his chin, studies them and sighs. 'A scratch might not be the same as a bite,' he says.

'But we can't take that chance,' Seez says quietly.

The Muslim sighs again. 'I'll head for the front door. If I make it, and if I don't turn, I'll try and get help for the rest of you.'

He darts through the doorway and is gone before Seez can say anything.

I glance at Pox and Dunglop one last time, my stomach turning, tears dripping down my cheeks. Then I swear hatefully and rush out after the others, leaving my dead and undead friends behind.

TWENTY

We pad along the corridor. Screams behind us, echoing, bouncing off the walls like they're never going to die away. I'm so glad I'm not in the gym. It sounds insane, way worse than when we snuck out.

At the end of the corridor we turn right. There are bodies sprawled across the floor. Students like us, scratched, torn, bitten, bloody. Dead. As we edge past, eyeing them nervously in case they spring to life, I note that their heads have been cracked open, their brains scooped out. Except one, a small girl whose skull is intact. The same can't be said for her guts—they're all over the place.

'Wait,' I whisper, stopping by the girl. I look for Cass. 'Give me your knife.'

'No one touches the knife but me,' he says coldly.

'Fine,' I snap. 'Then get over here and be ready to stab her in the head if she stirs.'

'What the hell are we waiting for?' Linzer snarls.

'I need to find out something.'

'Who do you think you are?' she screeches. 'Some sort of bloody –'

There's a creaking sound. Bones thrust through the tips of the dead girl's fingers, each at least a centimetre long. Her lips shake and pull back over her teeth, which are growing and getting thicker. Her arms writhe, then she sits up and hisses at us, hunger in her eyes. I shriek and fall back. She dives after me. Hooks my jumper with her fingers. Tries to dig in.

As I scream again, Cass appears by my side and drives his knife into the side of the girl's head, all the way to the hilt. She shivers, eyes rolling. He works the blade around, digs it in and out several times. The girl falls away from me and goes still.

I force myself to my feet and tug up my jumper and shirt, wildly examining my flesh for scratches, heart beating hard. The others are staring at me suspiciously. Cass's eyes are narrow, his fingers tight on the handle of the knife.

'Nothing,' I moan happily, exposing my stomach to them. 'She didn't cut me. See?'

168

'You're lucky,' Cass snorts.

'Now let's get the hell out of here, or do you want to study them some more?' Linzer sneers.

'I've confirmed what I wanted to.' I point at the other corpses. '*Brains*. Like in the movies. If they eat your brain, or if it's destroyed, you're properly dead and there's no coming back. That's how we kill them.'

'No shit, Sherlock,' Cass says. 'Now let's –'

La Lips screeches. A couple of bloodstained kids have stumbled into the corridor. Their eyes light up when they spot us and they stagger forward.

'Run!' I bark, and in a second we're racing past class-rooms and corpses.

The zombies follow silently. I shouldn't look back, but I can't help myself. I glance over my shoulder and spot them closing in. They're not smiling or leering. They don't pant either. They run expressionlessly, like robots. Only their eyes are alive.

One of the zombies grabs La Lips, who was strug-gling to keep up with the rest of us. She goes down with a yelp and it tears into her.

'Don't!' I shout at Copper as he stops to try and rescue her.

'I have to!' he yells and kicks at the zombie's head. The other one leaps on him. He bellows and lets fly with a flurry of punches. But the zombie pulls up Copper's jumper and bites into the soft flesh of his stomach. As Copper screams with pain and terror, the zombie rises, lips and teeth red, and comes after the rest of us again, leaving Copper to suffer, die and turn into one of the walking dead.

I want to help Copper and La Lips, but I can't. They're finished. No time to feel sorry for them. If the zombie grabs hold, I'm for the chop too. So I leg it, trying not to think about the friends I'm leaving behind. The poor, doomed friends that I've lost.

As we come to where the corridor branches, we turn left, but I steal a glance right then wish that I hadn't. There's another group of kids. Maybe they had the same idea as us and were making for the exit. But they've been set upon by a pack of zombies. They're trapped against a wall, dozens of transformed students holding them there, chewing through their skulls. The captured kids are screaming, sobbing, throwing up. All helpless. All damned.

A couple of zombies at the rear of the pack spot us and break away, joining the one who was already hot on our tail. They chase us down another corridor. The black kid whose name I don't know slips on a sliver of intestines. One of them is on him a moment later. He fights back manfully, but the zombie bites, scratches and pushes him down. We press on and leave him.

More corpses. The floor is sticky with blood. We dash past a room. The door's open. I spot a teacher inside, pinned to the whiteboard by four zombies. They're eating her, two on her arms, two on her legs, working their way up to her torso. She's alive and sobbing softly, her fingers, lips and eyelids spasming.

We come to a set of stairs. A few bodies lie spread-eagled across the steps. We clamber over them and up. But we can't all fit at once. It's a tight squeeze. Elbows and swear words fly as each of us struggles to be first to the top.

I'm next to Cass, the pair of us pushing forward, when he gives a cry of shock. I turn. The zombies have him. One's got his right leg, one the left. Both have bitten into his calves.

Cass screams and kicks at the zombies, but they hold firm. His eyes meet mine. He silently pleads with me to help him, do something, stop this. I shake my head numbly, then reach for his knife. He jerks it away from me.

'Please,' I whisper. 'It's no good to you now.'

Cass snarls at me and starts stabbing at the zombies. I watch him for a couple of seconds, then back away

slowly. Neither Cass nor the zombies pay any attention to me. They're locked in battle, but it's a fight that has only one of two possible outcomes. They tuck into his brain and he dies. Or they leave his skull alone and he becomes one of them. Either way, Cass is lost to us, so I wipe him from my thoughts as best I can and hobble up the stairs after the others.

TWENTY
-ONE

We pause at the top of the stairs to get our bearings. The two zombies below are still tucking into the screaming Cass and there are no others in sight.

'The exit's back that way,' Stagger Lee pants.

I'm familiar with it. I used it once in a fire drill. If we can get through the door, it leads, via a set of steps, to the same alley as the other emergency exit.

'Maybe we should make for the front of the building,' Trev says. 'We could jump from the windows.'

'This exit's closer,' Stagger Lee says.

'But if it's blocked . . .' Seez mutters.

'We've got to try,' Stagger Lee insists. 'It's our best hope.'

'Wait,' Tyler says. It's the first time he's spoken since we broke out of the gym. 'The canteen's over there.'

'You can't be hungry!' I gasp.

He shoots me a dirty look. 'They've got knives in the kitchen. We can tool up.'

I frown. That's not a bad idea. 'What about it?' I ask the group.

'Won't the canteen be full?' Suze asks. 'It's lunch, so it will be like the gym. If the zombies have struck there, it'll be bedlam.'

'But we'll have a much better chance if we have weapons,' Ballydefeck says.

'It's worth a look,' Elephant agrees.

'All right.' I nod at Tyler. 'Lead the way.'

'Me?' he squeaks.

I grin sharkishly. 'It was your idea. Only fair that if we get attacked, you should be first on their menu.'

It's hard to believe that I can make a joke at a time like this. But as awful as this is, as shocking as it's been, I can't shut down. At the moment I'm alive. Those of us in this group have a chance to get out and fight another day. We have to cling to life as tightly as we can, put the atrocities from our thoughts, deal with this as if it was a surprise exam. What I've learnt today is that when the shit hits the fan, you can sit around and get splattered,

176

or you can take it in your stride and do what you must to get away clean. I'll have nightmares about this later, maybe a full-on nervous breakdown, but only if I keep my cool and escape alive.

We follow Tyler along the corridors. We're the only ones on the move up here, none of the chaos of downstairs. I have visions of walking into the canteen, everyone eating, unaware of what's happening below. Maybe they'll think we're winding them up. They might ignore our warnings and carry on with their lunch, oblivious until the zombies come crashing in on them.

But when we get there, I immediately see that reality has struck just as hard in the canteen as it has downstairs. In fact it's struck even harder.

Students, along with some teachers and kitchen staff, are backed up against one of the walls. They're moaning and sobbing, but hardly any of them are fighting or trying to break free. They seem to have abandoned hope completely.

They're surrounded by scores of zombies, maybe a hundred or more. They're picking off the living one by one, biting some to convert them, tearing into the brains of others. It's a carefully organised operation. And pulling the strings, directing the movements of the undead, is a small group of men and women in hoodies.

My breath catches in my throat. We're watching from outside the canteen, through two round windows in the doors, taking turns to observe the horror show. But when my turn comes and I spot the people in the hoodies, I freeze and can't be torn away.

There are several of them. Each has a whistle, which they blow every now and then to command attention. They have rotten skin, pockmarked with pustulent sores, purple in places, patches of flesh peeling away. All have grey, lifeless hair and pale yellow eyes. I can't see inside their mouths, but I'm pretty sure that if I examined them close up, I'd find shrivelled, scabby tongues.

They're the same type of creeps as the two guys at the Imperial War Museum, the mutants who tried to kidnap the baby. And they're clearly in control, dominating the zombies, using them to process the survivors neatly and efficiently.

Seez was right. This isn't bad luck or a freak attack. We've been set up. And even though I wouldn't have believed it was possible a minute ago, I feel even more fear now than I did when the zombies first burst into the gym.

TWENTY
-TWO

We head for the exit, numb and dumb with shock. I
don't think anyone now expects it to be open. But we
act as if we hadn't seen the slaughter in the canteen, as
if we don't know what it means.

We're at the door a minute later. We stare at the bar.
If it works, and the door opens, we're just seconds away
from freedom.

Nobody reaches for the bar. Everyone's afraid of being
the one to fail, to dash the hope which we all long for,
but don't dare believe in. Finally I sigh and step up to
the challenge. I push the bar down. It clicks. I pause a
second, then push.

Nothing happens.

I close my eyes and lean my head against the door. Then I swear and push again, straining, putting everything into it. But I'm wasting my time. It doesn't budge.

'B,' Trev says.

I fire one of my vilest swear words his way.

'B,' he says calmly. 'Look.'

I turn and spot something on the floor to our left. I clocked it before, but thought it was just a corpse. Now I see that there are actually two bodies. And one of them's moving, chewing on the head of the other, slurping down brains.

As we stare with disgust, the zombie pushes its victim away and stands. We all gasp at the same time.

'Mrs Reed!' I shout.

The zombie which was once our principal sways from side to side, staring at us blankly, chin drenched with blood and flecked with bits of brain. I get a fix on the body beneath her and cringe. It's Jonesenzio. He won't be boring anyone with dry history lectures again. Poor old sod.

Mrs Reed shuffles towards us. Nobody moves. She doesn't seem to pose an immediate threat. She's smiling stupidly, eyes unfocused, rubbing her stomach. She burps and giggles softly.

'This is unreal,' the Indian kid sighs.

Mrs Reed's eyes settle on him and she frowns. She raises a finger and shakes it slowly. Then she spots me. Her smile spreads again.

'*Beeeeeeee*,' she wheezes.

'Bloody hell!' Elephant yelps. 'How's she talking? Zombies can't talk! Can they?'

Mrs Reed comes closer. She's within touching distance of me now, but I can't move. I'm rooted. The others back up, but nobody runs or screams or tries to pull me away from her. They're mesmerised, held captive by the spectacle like I am.

Mrs Reed strokes my cheek with a finger – there's no bone sticking out of it – and leaves a trail of blood across my flesh. But she doesn't scratch me and claim me for one of her own. Her eyes are locked on mine. She looks demented, but strangely peaceful at the same time.

'*Fullll*,' she whispers, still rubbing her stomach with her other hand.

'What's happening?' Seez asks, distracting her. 'Where did the zombies come from? Who are the freaks in the hoodies? Who locked the doors?'

Mrs Reed snarls at him. Then she smiles at me again and taps the side of my head. '*Stayyy. Hungry again . . . sooooon.*'

'Sorry,' I croak, stepping away from her. 'I don't fancy being eaten.'

Mrs Reed looks disappointed, but she shrugs and sits down. Dabs at the bits of brain stuck to her chin and sucks them from her finger.

I'm backing away from the zombie principal when I stop. This isn't right. She's not like any of the others we've encountered. And it's not just the fact that she can talk and doesn't have bones sticking out of her fingers. There are no bite marks or scratches. I can't see where she was wounded.

I want to study her properly – this seems important – but Trev interrupts.

'We have to get out of here.'

'But this is weird,' I argue. 'She's different. I want to know why.'

Trev shrugs. 'Then stay and have a chat with her. Me, I'm heading for the front of the building, to get the hell out. They might have barred the doors, but they can't have blocked all the windows. There wasn't enough time.'

'He's right,' Seez says. 'The windows are our best hope.'

'You don't have any hope,' someone snickers behind us.

I whirl and spot three people in hoodies. They're spread across the corridor, grinning viciously. I'm almost certain that the one in the middle is the louse who tried to steal the baby in the museum. Then he points at me and says, 'You should have let me take the boy,' and my suspicions are confirmed.

'Who are you?' I yell. 'Why are you doing this?'

'Don't worry,' the mutant chuckles, his voice gravelly and gurgly, nothing like a normal person's. 'You're in good company. This is happening all over London. This will be a city of zombies by the time the sun sets. And it won't be the only one. From tomorrow, this world is ours.'

As we stare at the mutant with the crazy skin and yellow eyes, horrified by his prediction, he puts his whistle to his lips and blows. The others blow their whistles too. Three long, sharp toots. They're so piercing, I have to cover my ears with my hands. Then the mutants drop the whistles and smirk. Lowering my hands, I fix on the sound of a flurry of feet stomping down the corridor, dozens of zombies responding to the call of the mutants, closing in on *us*.

TWENTY -THREE

No time to think. We run from the mob of zombies, tear along the corridor, knowing we don't have much time.

As we pass an open door to a classroom, Linzer ducks inside. 'I'm hiding!' she screams, slamming the door shut on the rest of us.

Meths starts to slow, but Stagger Lee bellows at him, 'Leave her!'

We press on. My heart's hammering. I'm finding it hard to breathe. I was never the fittest—too many helpings of chips and not enough exercise. I start to drift towards the rear of the group. We turn a corner, then another. I've lost track of where we are. The zombies are drawing closer. The mutants in hoodies must be with them because I hear an occasional whistle.

I'm rushing past a window when I catch a glimpse of open space. I stop and yell to the others, 'We're next to a courtyard. I'm jumping.'

'We don't know what's down there,' Trev roars. 'It could be full of zombies.'

I grin ghoulishly. 'Only one way to find out.' I back up from the window, then hurl myself at the glass, covering my face with my arms. There's a good chance I'll slice open a vein or artery, but I'd rather bleed to death than be devoured by the living dead.

I smash through the window and whoop insanely, half terrified, half buzzing. My arms snap open and flap wildly. A brief glimpse of the ground coming fast towards me. Then I land in an untidy heap and roll awkwardly. The air's knocked out of me. Shards of glass nick my hands and knees. But I'm alive. I'm not badly injured. And the courtyard's empty.

'Come on!' I shout at the others.

Seez follows first, bursting through another pane of glass. There's a wide hole now and the rest can jump cleanly. They pile after us, landing hard, picking themselves up, a few cuts and bruises, but no broken ankles or severed arteries.

Suze and Ballydefeck are last. Suze stares at the drop with terror. She's crying.

'Hurry up,' Ballydefeck says, grabbing her.

She shakes him off. 'I can't. I'm afraid of heights.'

'It's not that bloody high!'

'I –'

A scream from a window on the other side of the courtyard stops her. We all look. Linzer is pressed against the glass, her face contorted. Zombies are bunched around her. They yank her out of sight. Looks like Cass might have been right about them having a keen nose for the living.

'Get down and drop then,' Ballydefeck barks, getting to his knees and backing out, holding onto the sill.

'All right,' Suze moans, shutting her eyes. 'But I can't look. You tell me where I have to –'

There's a blur of motion. A zombie tackles Suze and she's gone before she can scream. Ballydefeck yelps and lets go. But hands snake out and grab his arms. He's hauled back into the room, roaring and cursing.

Several zombies lean out through the shattered windows and I'm sure they're going to jump and finish us off. But the sunlight unnerves them. They wince, cover their eyes and back away into the gloom. Before hungrier or braver zombies can take their place, we find the nearest door and race back inside, stumbling slightly, feet stinging from the jump, but delighted to be alive, all too aware that we could have very easily gone the same way as Linzer, Suze and Ballydefeck.

TWENTY -FOUR

Nine of us left. Me, Trev, Meths, Elephant, Stagger Lee, Tyler, Seez, the other Muslim boy and the Indian. As we run, twisting through corridors, I try to remember how many of us there were to begin with, but I can't. I've already forgotten the names and faces of the dead. I'm sure, if I sat down for five minutes, I'd be able to recall them. But right now they're vaguely remembered ghosts.

Sounds behind us again. The zombies must have overcome their fear of the light. The chase has resumed.

'Hold on,' Trev pants, coming to a stop. 'Where are we? I don't know if we're heading back towards the gym or close to the front.'

We gaze around. There are classrooms on both sides, but I don't recognise them. All of the corridors have started to look the same. I'm as lost as Trev. By the blank stares of the others, I know that they are too.

Tyler coughs shyly and points. 'The front's that way.'

'You're sure?' Trev asks.

'Yeah,' he says with a small smile. 'I'm good at directions, me.'

'Then let's go.'

We head the way Tyler pointed. He'd better be right. If he's not, I'll kill him before the zombies can.

We turn a corner and I run into a boy my own size. We collide, bounce off each other and fall. Sitting up and rubbing my head, I realise it's Pox and I burst into a smile.

'Pox! I thought you were . . .'

I stop. Pox is staring at me with a hungry look. I remember that the last time I saw him, he was dining on Dunglop's brain. My eyes flash to the fingers of his left hand and I see a light green moss running along the bite marks. Bones jut nastily from the ruined tips of his fingers.

Rick's just behind Pox. He's limping, dragging one

leg. His foot's missing. Pox or another zombie must have chewed it off before he turned. But there's not much blood.

Pox scuttles after me. Dunglop's brain obviously wasn't enough to satisfy his appetite. Like Meths, poor old Dunglop never was the brightest of sparks, so he must have made for no more than a snack.

I kick at Pox's face, driving him back. As I try to scramble to my feet, Meths wades in and kicks Pox harder. Rick hops towards Meths, arms wide, fingers flexed like a cat's claws. Meths slips. Rick ducks in for the kill –

– then there's an unnatural roar and the zombie flies backwards, stomach ripped to shreds, blood spattering the wall and floor behind him.

Pox gets up and snarls. Goes for me again. There's another roar and his head explodes. Somebody's firing bullets. Someone has a gun.

Bloody *yes,* mate!

'His head!' I roar as Rick hobbles forward, guts spilling down his legs. 'Shoot him in the head! That's the only way to stop them!'

The gun fires again and Rick's temple cracks open. He drops in a lifeless heap.

I turn to face the gunman. The others have all turned

too, jaws slack, hardly able to believe that this is real. I'm hoping for a squadron of soldiers, but it's just a normal-looking guy with a rifle. He hasn't lowered it and is staring grimly down the barrel at *me*.

'Were you bitten?' he growls.

'No!' I scream.

'Don't lie. I saw it attack you. Stand back!' he barks at the others.

I gawp at the man with the gun. This is so unfair. To survive the zombies, only to be finished off by an idiot who won't listen. I'd love to knock some sense into his thick head. But it doesn't look like I'll have a chance, because he's aiming at the middle of my face. Any second now he's gonna –

'Stop!' another man roars. 'Don't shoot! That's my daughter!'

'But I saw –' the man with the rifle begins.

The rest of what he says is lost to me. Because suddenly Dad is there, pushing past the idiot with the gun, spreading his arms wide, stooping to hug me.

'Dad!' I cry with a rush of relief.

'*Becky*!' he moans, wrapping his arms round me and hugging me tight. 'My girl! My girl!'

Then he's kissing me and hugging me, and I don't care how many zombies or idiots with trigger-happy

fingers there are. They can't hurt me. They don't matter any more. Dad loves me. He risked his life to find me. Everything will be all right now. Dad will save me. He'll save us all. He's a bloody hero!

TWENTY
-FIVE

'Todd,' the man with the gun says, interrupting our hug fest. Dad looks up, happy tears sparkling in his eyes, grinning like a loon. 'Our kids aren't here. We have to push on.'

Dad's grin fades. He pats my head, then stands. The two men shake hands. There are a couple of women behind the guy with the gun, one white, one Chinese. Dad smiles sadly at the white woman, but only scowls at the other one.

'You're sure you want to continue?' Dad asks Gun Guy.

'I have to.' He turns to the rest of us. 'Any of you know Jimmy Wilkins?' Most of us nod. 'Have you seen him?' We shake our heads.

'What about Lindsay Hogan?' the white woman asks.

Linzer.

'The zombies got her,' I mutter.

The woman's face hardens. 'No!' she snaps. 'You're wrong.'

'We saw them grab her.'

'Where?' she screams.

I turn and point. The woman starts running. 'It was on the top floor,' I shout. 'You're too late. She's dead.'

But the woman isn't listening. She's gone.

The Chinese woman asks us if we've seen her son and daughter, but we don't know either of them. She heads off with Gun Guy, the pair advancing swiftly, checking each room as they pass.

'It's madness,' I whisper to Dad. 'They're gonna get killed.'

'I know, love,' he says. 'But that's what parents do for their kids. I knew I'd probably get eaten when I came looking for you, but did that stop me? Did it hell.'

I beam at him, so proud. He looks around, smiles at my friends, sniffs at the Muslims, the Indian and Tyler. 'Come on,' he says. 'I'm getting you out of here.'

We follow Dad back the way he came. He's moving quickly, but he isn't racing. 'Slow down,' he says as Trev tries to force the pace.

'But the zombies . . .' Trev gasps.

'You think I don't know about them?' Dad snorts.

'We have to get out,' Trev insists.

'That's what we're doing,' Dad says calmly. 'But if we go flapping around like headless chickens, we'll run into trouble, the way you lot did before I found you. These zombies aren't so tough if you're prepared for them. I've finished off a few of them already.' He shakes a metal bar at us—it's red with blood. 'But you have to go about it the right way, keep your head, make sure you have the time and space to spot them coming.'

He takes a left turn and we pass the staffroom. The door's open. I spot a couple of teachers inside, chewing on the remains of some of their colleagues.

'They won't be failing you again,' Dad says and we both laugh.

'Straight Fs in most courses,' I chuckle. 'But A+ in zombie survival!'

'Been a long time since I was a student here,' Dad mutters nostalgically. 'But I remember the place like it was yesterday. Didn't have any trouble finding my way around.'

'How'd you get over here so quickly?' I ask. It feels like we've been running for hours since the gym, but it can't have been more than fifteen or twenty minutes.

'I was working nearby,' Dad says. 'When I heard about the attacks on the radio, I ran like the wind. I tried ringing ahead to check if things were all right, but the phones aren't working.'

'Then it's true?' Elephant asks. 'This is happening in other places too?'

'Yeah,' Dad says. 'Schools, hospitals, shops, factories, all sorts. Getting out of here won't be the end of it. London's in uproar. But the zombies tend to keep to the shadows. If we stick to the main streets and roads, we should be all right. At least until night.'

'What about Mum?' I ask, able to think about her now that I have someone else to watch out for me.

'We'll swing by home, see if she's there,' Dad says.

'Can't we ring and get her to –'

'Weren't you listening?' he snaps. 'The phones are dead. Mobiles, landlines, the lot. TV stations are down too. A lot of radio stations as well, but a guy I work with has a top-of-the-range set that picks up a huge variety of frequencies. That's how I know it's widespread. It started about . . .' He checks his watch. 'Not quite an hour ago. But I didn't hear about it immediately. As soon as I did, I came.' He flashes me a shaky smile. 'You didn't think I'd leave you to be gobbled by zombies, did you?'

I want to burst into tears and hug him again, but

there's no time. We have to keep moving. We'll be relatively safe in the sunlight once we get out of here. We can hug all we want then.

We move steadily through the school, drawing closer to the front of the building. For the first time since the gym I really allow myself to hope. I don't want to tempt fate, but I think we've made it.

We come to a corridor that's only a few turns from the main exit. Everyone's excited. We can virtually smell freedom. There's a fire door ahead of us. Once we push through that, the corridor branches. The right turn leads back into the school. The left will lead us all the way home.

Dad shoves the door. It rattles but doesn't open. He frowns and pushes it again. No joy. 'That's not right,' he says. 'I came through here on my way in.'

The Indian kid slides up to the crack in the door and peers through. 'It's been locked,' he moans. 'There's a chain.'

'What?' Dad shouts, shoving him aside and squinting through the crack. 'Who the hell did that?'

'The mutants,' I sigh. As if in answer, I hear a whistle blow somewhere close behind us. 'Dad! They're coming!'

Dad stares at me. He starts to ask how I know we're

in trouble, then shakes his head and slams the door with his shoulder. 'Keep back,' he grunts at those around him. 'It'll take more than a chain to hold *me* here.'

We stare at Dad as he rams the door again and again. It's a thick, heavy door, designed to slow the spread of flames in case of a fire. The chain is sturdy too. Dad doesn't look to be achieving much, but he keeps going, sweating like a marathon runner, totally focused.

I glance back down the corridor and spot four zombies slipping into it. They lock sights on us and slither forward.

'Dad!' I wail.

'I nearly have it,' he pants.

Trev throws himself at the door, trying to help. Meths and Seez take turns too. Dad glares at them, but then there's a snapping sound and the door starts to give. 'That's the way, boys!' Dad whoops. 'Give it everything you have.'

They hurl themselves at the door, one after the other. Their arms and shoulders will be black and blue later, but they don't care. No matter how much of a battering they take, they don't back down.

Elephant, Stagger Lee, the Indian and the other Muslim kid watch helplessly as Dad and the three boys fly at the door like rabid dogs. I'm a bit further back,

Tyler by my side. I'm looking for anything I can use to fend off the zombies, but I'm not having much luck. They're closing in. They could have rushed us by now, but they see that we're trapped, so they're taking their time.

'Dad!' I yell.

'Just another few blows,' he wheezes, launching himself at the door again.

More zombies appear at the far end of the corridor, loads of them, a couple of whistle-blowing mutants in the middle, guiding them towards us.

'*Dad!*'

Dad looks back and whitens. 'Holy hell,' he croaks.

Meths bangs into the door and it cracks. The hinges give. Meths cheers and starts shaking the door. Dad and Seez join him. There isn't room for Trev—he's been pushed out of the way.

'They're almost on us,' I shout.

Dad looks at me, then at the zombies, and swears. 'You've got to stall them. We only need a few more seconds.'

'How?' I scream. 'There's nothing I can do to –'

'Throw them the black kid!' Dad roars.

I stare at him. Tyler stares too, both of us stunned, momentarily forgetting about the zombies.

'Do it!' Dad shouts.

'But he's Tyler,' I whisper. 'He's one of us. He helped us get –'

'Throw them the bloody chimneysweep or I'll whip you raw!' Dad screams.

And suddenly I'm reacting, doing what he tells me, the way I always do when he loses his temper, because it's easier to obey him than stand up to him. Years of conditioning kick in. Fear takes over. I go into my dutiful daughter act. The racist in me swims to the fore and rejoices at being set free.

On autopilot, I grab Tyler's arm and whirl him at the zombies.

'*No!*' he shrieks as he stumbles towards them. 'B! No! Help me!'

Tyler crashes into the zombies. All five go down and the zombies sprawl like bowling pins. Tyler starts to get up. Immediately guilt-stricken and appalled, I reach out to him, desperately wanting to put right what I've done. But before I can drag him to safety, a zombie catches hold and bites Tyler's neck. Tyler chokes and stiffens, blood spurting, and I watch with horror as the other three zombies crowd around and tuck into the tasty human morsel that I've thrown them.

TWENTY
- SIX

I've seen a lot of terrible things today, but nothing compares with this. It's not that Tyler dies more horribly than any of the others who've been torn to pieces. But *I* sacrificed him. I let Dad bully me, the way I've always done, and now a boy is dead because of it. Because of *me*.

As the other zombies draw closer, the scent of Tyler's blood luring them on, Dad jerks the door open and bellows triumphantly. Trev and the others squeeze through. Dad dashes back and pulls me away from the awful spectacle of Tyler Bayor being finished off by the undead.

'Come on,' Dad pants. 'We've got to get out of here.'

Dad shoves the Indian kid away from the door and growls at him, 'Get out of it, Gandhi. My daughter goes first.'

He shoves me through, then follows. The Indian boy's squealing. He tries to wriggle after us, but a zombie grabs him. He screeches and reaches out to us, pleading to be saved. Dad sneers, then pushes him back and slams the door shut.

'Help me hold this,' he snaps at Trev and Meths. They obey without question, shocked into submission by his viciousness, dominated by the cruelty in his voice, the same way I've been dominated by it all my life.

Dad looks around for something to jam the door with, but there's nothing. 'All right,' he pants, straining with Trev and Meths to hold back the zombies. 'I'm guessing they'll pile up and get stuck. It'll take them a while to sort themselves out. You lot run ahead. We'll hold this a bit longer, then dash after you and hope we get enough of a start on them.'

Elephant, Stagger Lee, Seez and the other Muslim boy peel away to the left. They're crying and shaking, but they push on, freedom all but guaranteed now.

'Go on, B,' Dad says.

I shake my head.

'Stupid girl,' he mutters, then winces as the door buckles. 'All right, stick with me then. Are you two ready? We'll let go on the count of three.'

Trev and Meths nod nervously. Then Dad shouts swiftly, 'One two three!'

The trio release the door and make a break for it. The zombies push hard on the door and it tears free. But like Dad guessed, too many try to squeeze through at the same time and they get jammed. It'll be a few seconds before they make any headway.

Dad realises I'm not with him. He pauses and turns. Sees me backing away. 'B!' he shouts. 'What the hell are you doing?'

'I can't,' I moan.

He starts towards me. Stops when he spots the zombies untangling themselves. 'Come on!' he screams, extending a hand. 'I didn't go through all this to lose you now. Get your arse over here before –'

'You know the problem with you, Dad?' I stop him, calmer than I've any right to be, wiping angry, bitter tears from my cheeks. 'You're a bigger monster than any bloody zombie.'

As Dad gawps at me, bewildered, I turn my back on the man I love more than any in the world, the man I hate more than any in the world, and stumble away from him, from the exit, from safety. As he roars my name, I follow the branch of the corridor that leads back into the building, preferring to take my chances among the zombies than go along with the racist beast who made me kill Tyler Bayor.

TWENTY -SEVEN

Twisting and turning, racing along corridors, tears streaming down my face. I pant and stumble, but never fall or falter. Never look back either, afraid of what I might see, zombies or Dad, one as bad as the other.

I can't believe I'm doing this. I was so close to freedom. I should have escaped with the others, dealt with Dad outside, fought my fight when my life wasn't on the line.

But I couldn't. For all these years I've said nothing when he hit Mum, when he hit me, when he demonised anyone who wasn't white. I never stood up to him. I put on an act, tried to pretend it didn't matter.

And not just because I was afraid of him. Because I loved him too. He was my dad. I didn't want to admit that he was truly evil, irredeemably warped.

But he turned me into a killer. He made me throw Tyler to the zombies. I can't forgive that. I can't lie to myself, dismiss it as an isolated incident, tell myself that he'll change. Tyler and I weren't close, he wasn't a friend, but he helped us get as far as we did. We might not have found our way out without him. He didn't deserve to be killed because of the colour of his skin. Nor the Indian boy, sacrificed by a man who cares for nobody except his own.

I remember something that Mr Burke said a while back. *There are lots of black-hearted, mean-spirited bastards in the world. It's important that we hold them to account. But always remember that* you *might be the most black-hearted and mean-spirited of the lot, so hold yourself the most accountable of all.*

I've played a cringing neutral all my life, and it turned me into something far worse than I ever feared I'd become. But that changes here, today, now. If I get out of this alive, I'll never make a mistake like that again. I can't bring Tyler back – that will haunt me forever, and nothing can ever make up for it – but from this point on I'll do whatever I can to stand up to Dad and anyone like him. I swear on the blood I've shed, on the life I've destroyed.

I come to an intersection and turn right, but there are zombies shambling up the corridor towards me. I backpedal and push on straight. The zombies give chase.

I'm passing a room when a girl staggers out ahead of me. She's bleeding, one arm bitten off at the elbow. A zombie follows, a boy my size, his clothes almost torn to shreds. He decides I'm richer pickings and makes a grab for me.

I duck, but not quickly enough. Fingerbones rake my arm and catch on the exposed flesh of my wrist. I yelp and kick at him. He snaps for my leg with his teeth, but I pull it back in time. Kick him hard in the head. Race on.

I stare at the scratch as I run, terror mounting. We never found out whether a scratch was enough to turn a human into a zombie. Maybe it's harmless and they can only convert by biting, a transfer of saliva or blood. But I wouldn't bet on it. I think it's all over for me. In another minute or two I'll probably throw up like Pox did, give a shiver and a grunt, and never think clearly again.

I come to a set of stairs and start up the steps, figuring I can get to the windows at the front and jump to safety. I have to believe it's not too late. If I can get out of the school, maybe I can be helped, even if the scratch *is* infectious. I'm hoping it isn't, but if it is, maybe someone can chop off my arm or inject me with a cure or ... or ... *something*. It doesn't matter that I'm clutching at straws. Better I cling to some kind of hope than abandon it entirely.

But I'm not halfway up the steps when even the thinnest sliver of hope is ripped away from me forever.

'Run, run as fast as you can,' someone gurgles ahead of me.

I look up and spot the mutant from the museum, the one I ran into earlier. There are dozens of zombies behind him, staring at me, drooling, fingers twitching, awaiting the order to attack.

I come to a halt and stare at the man with the yellow eyes and purplish skin. He's giggling sickly. 'Where are you going, Becky?' he crows.

I take a step back, whimpering softly, looking for angles, seeing nothing but zombies. I feel dizzy and nauseous. Am I turning or is it just fear?

'I was scratched,' I moan, holding out my hand, eyesight blurring, senses going into a tailspin. 'Does that mean ...?'

The mutant cackles. 'Yes. But you've more than a

scratch to worry about. It looks to me like one of your friends wants a word.'

He nods at the stairs behind me. I turn and find Tyler standing on the step just below mine. His chin is lowered. Blood and a light green layer of moss cakes his shoulder and neck, and all the other places where he was bitten. I can't see his eyes.

Before I can say anything, Tyler's right hand shoots forward. His fingers are stiff, hooked slightly, the bones at the tips sticking out like small daggers. They hammer into my chest, shatter my breastbone, clasp round my heart. As I scream with shock and agony, Tyler rips my heart free of my body. I see it pulse in his palm a few times. Then he rams it into his mouth, tears off a chunk and swallows.

That's the last thing I see in this life, Tyler chewing on my heart, grinning viciously—revenge is obviously as sweet as people always said it was.

Then I'm falling, fading away. The world goes black around the edges, throbs, and all is consumed by a wave of dark nothingness.

I die.

To be continued . . .